A
Harlequin
Romance

OTHER
Harlequin Romances
by ELIZABETH ASHTON

Many of these titles are available at your local bookseller,
or through the Harlequin Reader Service.

For a free catalogue listing all available Harlequin Romances,
send your name and address to:

HARLEQUIN READER SERVICE,
M.P.O. Box 707; Niagara Falls, N.Y. 14302
Canadian address: Stratford, Ontario, Canada N5A 6W4

or use coupon at back of books.

MISS NOBODY
FROM NOWHERE

by

ELIZABETH ASHTON

HARLEQUIN BOOKS   TORONTO
WINNIPEG

Original hard cover edition published in 1975
by Mills & Boon Limited

SBN 373-01933-5

Harlequin edition published December 1975

Printed in Canada

1933

CHAPTER ONE

THE girl opened her eyes and stared bewildered around the room in which she was lying, for it was unlike any place in which she had ever been before. It was a small room with wooden walls and a floor of beaten earth and was warmed by a charcoal brazier. She found that she was lying on a narrow bed and covered by several quilts, for in spite of the heat from the stove, chilly draughts circulated through the room. Her eyes sought the small square of window, which showed a blinding whiteness outside, which was reflected upon the ceiling. Snow, she registered vaguely; wherever she was it must be winter. She began to take in the details of the furniture, seeking a familiar object. It was crude—a table, some pottery utensils, a handwoven rug by the bed, and a pile of cushions in one corner covered in leather. There was a single chair, and this surprisingly was ornately carved in an archaic design, being of the shape described as 'Hamlet'.

She knitted her brows in the effort to remember what had happened, and came up against a veil of darkness. Dimly she was aware that it concealed some tragedy, but what that was she could not recollect. She must have been ill, for she realised that she was very weak. The mere attempt to lift herself on the bed caused her head to swim and she sank back defeated. She discovered one ankle was bandaged and her shoulder ached. Curiously she looked at her hands; they looked white and frail as she laid them on the quilt, and pitifully useless. She noticed that she wore no rings. Her long black hair was neatly braided in two long plaits, one over each shoulder. She was wearing a sort of chemise made of fine white wool—not, she was sure, her usual choice of a nightgown. She must have met with an accident and this was a hospital, but it appeared to be a very primitive one. Again she tried to remember, but the veil would not lift, and her memory remained a complete blank. All she knew was that she was alive and in an unknown place.

The crude wooden door opened and a man and a woman came in. The woman wore a long full skirt and a shawl with a scarf over her head. She was old and wrinkled with faded blue eyes. She stood deferentially to one side to allow the man to pass her on his way to the bed. She remained standing by the door, and the girl was only aware of her as a hovering bulky shadow.

The man was different. He radiated virile strength, causing the girl to sink back on her pillows, overwhelmed by his magnetic presence. He was not very tall, but he seemed to fill the little room, and he loomed over her like a giant, his size being due in part to his clothes, which had been chosen to withstand bitter weather; they consisted of baggy trousers thrust into high skin boots, some sort of wool tunic, and a cloak lined with fur. But it was his head which drew her attention, for it was arresting. Under a karacul cap, his golden hair reached to his shoulders to join whiskers and beard, also golden, which gave him the appearance of an old-time Viking. All she could discern of his features was a straight nose, with a haughty curl of nostril, and penetrating grey eyes, set beneath a finely moulded brow and thick fair eyebrows.

The girl looked up at him in faint astonishment, sure now that she was in the throes of some fantastic dream, while, he, seeing that she was awake, addressed her in an unknown tongue, while his fingers sought for her pulse. An electric current shot up her arm at his touch, which was both unnerving and invigorating. Weakly she tried to withdraw her wrist from those strong, brown fingers, while she murmured fainly:

'Where am I? What has happened?'

'So you've recovered consciousness at last,' he said with satisfaction in her own tongue. He released her wrist and stepped back. 'Are you English, or American?'

She regarded him with a faint frown.

'I don't know.'

The grey eyes became more intent.

'You don't know?' he asked gently. 'You mean you can't tell us who you are and where you come from?'

Again she knitted her fine black brows in the effort to remember, but the impenetrable veil refused to lift. With a feeling of horror, she realised that she had lost her identity together with all recollection of her past. Tears of desperation rose to her eyes and trickled down her wan cheeks, as she murmured forlornly:

'It's all gone, my mind is just a blank.'

He knelt beside the bed, and taking her hand stroked it reassuringly.

'Don't distress yourself,' he bade her kindly. 'It's only temporary amnesia, the result of shock. Everything will come back to you in time. Meanwhile, you must rest and nurse your strength.' She continued to weep, for she was very weak, and pulling a handkerchief from a pocket, he wiped her eyes as tenderly as a mother wipes those of a sick child. 'Don't cry, you're among friends, we will take good care of you.'

Gradually her sobs subsided, and she asked anxiously:

'Was I in an accident?'

He hesitated, then told her: 'Well, yes, you could call it that.'

So she was in some sort of hospital, but the rugged figure kneeling beside her did not look like that of a doctor. She enquired:

'Haven't I got any friends or relations who are asking for me?'

Again he hesitated. 'This is rather a remote spot,' he informed her at length, 'and since winter has set in, communications with the outside world are ... difficult.'

'Then where am I?'

'Actually the village hasn't got a name, but don't worry your head about anything, just sleep. You've talked enough for the first time.' He patted her hand and laid it back inside the quilt. 'We will do all we can to trace your friends. Now Aziza will bring you some warm milk, and when you wake up again, perhaps you will remember.'

'Tell me first who you are?'

'My name is Clive Stratton. I'm an anthropologist, and I'm spending the winter here to study the people and their way of life. Fortunately for you, since I also am British.'

He signed to the woman, who quietly withdrew.

The girl closed her eyes and lay still, already exhausted by this brief encounter and thankful to let her problems rest. The man rose to his feet and stood looking down at her compassionately. Her face was very white between her plaits of inky hair and long black lashes concealed the eyes which had looked at him so despairingly. Eventually he would have to tell her that

8

she was the only survivor of an air crash in the valley. The plane in which she was travelling had wandered off course and apparently had struck a rocky peak, concealed in the low clouds. It had fallen into a ravine from which it would be almost impossible to extricate its remains, if there were any, but from the cloud of smoke that had ascended from the aperture, it would seem to have caught fire. By some freakish chance, the girl had been thrown out when the plane had disintegrated on to a ledge of rock which overhung the ravine, but no other survivors had been found, and there could be none in that almost bottomless crevasse. The traumatic experience had robbed her of her memory, possibly aggravated by other stresses she had undergone before the accident. The mind can bear so much and no more, then it builds up its own defences. Amnesia was infinitely preferable to madness.

She would retain the memory of normal actions, speech and the habits of everyday life, for this was ingrained knowledge that functioned automatically. A spoon in her hand would remind her how to use it, a printed page would mechanically be read; only the effort of recollection was beyond her, but at any moment some association with her past might bring it back to her.

Clive Stratton was not a qualified doctor, but he had studied medicine, knowing that such knowledge would be an asset to him during his travels through the inaccessible parts of the earth that he liked to explore, but he had never anticipated that he would number a British girl among his patients, and one who had lost her memory. For from her speech she was undoubtedly British with no trace of accent or Americanisms. He smiled wryly as he studied the pale face below him. The white light from the snow outside illuminated it, the features looking like carved ivory, they were delicately formed and definitely Nordic. The beautiful mouth drooped at the corners; she was unhappy and would be more so when she learned the fate of the plane. Who had she been travelling with, father, husband, or lover? Impulsively he picked up her left hand and saw as she had done that it was ringless.

Aziza returned with a bowl of warm goat's milk and made a slight obeisance. The big golden-haired man was to her a demi-god. She was a sturdy mountain woman, but deference to the male had been taught by her people for generations and in spite of modern teaching which was spreading even into Asia, it would take many years for it to die out, and the villagers were Moslems.

Clive dropped the girl's hand, aware that Aziza was regarding him slyly. Already her people had put their own interpretation upon the white girl's surprising advent. To their simple minds, the doctor was a superman with his great powers of endurance and his medical skill. He had come to them out of the blue and hospitality demanded he must be made welcome, and they had been rewarded, for he had effected many cures. But Allah knew men should not live alone, and since such a great personage naturally scorned the village girls, the Omnipotent One had in his inscrutable wisdom sent a mate for him literally down from heaven. Only it was a pity he had not delivered her in better condition.

Clive was well aware of their reasoning, and had made no demur when they had assigned a house to him and his patient, after her timely rescue from the rocks. It was convenient to have her in the room next to his, for at first it had seemed she would die and she needed all his skill by night and day, and accepting her as a challenge to it, he had had only one aim, to endeavour to save her. Now that she was recovering, she might prove to be a complication; he did not want a wife.

Aziza bent over the bed, raising the girl's head to take the milk, and with an impatient exclamation Clive strode out of the room, as she opened her dark eyes and looked at him appealingly.

The valley where the plane had met its doom was one of the many almost unknown settlements in the inaccessible regions of the Hindu Kush called Nuristan. Its people had intrigued Clive Stratton, for their origins were still mysterious and they were unlike any of their neighbours, though officially a part of Afghanistan, for Abdur Rahman had subdued them in the nineteenth century and annexed their territory. But they continued to isolate themselves, and rarely was a Nuristani to be met with in other provinces.

Already internationally celebrated for his research among obscure peoples—the Tuaregs of the Sahara, the Amazonian Indians, the Iranian nomads—Clive had come to Nuristan intending to spend the winter there studying the customs and origins of its inhabitants, and now found himself saddled with a girl who could not remember who she was.

From the day upon which she regained consciousness, the girl's condition began to improve rapidly. She had no broken bones, though one ankle had been badly sprained and her shoulder dislocated. She had suffered most from cold and exposure. It was a Nuristani shepherd who had found her and brought her in, but it was Clive who had ministered to her when she appeared nearly dead, spooning milk tinctured with spirits between her lips to revive the feeble spark of life that still flickered within her inert body. Beyond

11

doubt she owed him her life, but whether she was to thank him for that or otherwise had yet to be revealed.

He visited her every morning and evening, while in the interim Aziza attended to her wants. On the third day after her awakening, he considered that she was strong enough to be told about the air crash.

She received the news without distress, for though it accounted for her presence, she had no recollection of any of the crew or passengers.

'A dreadful thing to happen,' she commented, but without feeling personally involved, adding meditatively: 'I suppose I must have been with someone.'

'I hardly think you'd be roaming this wild land alone.'

'If only I could remember whom!'

But did she really want to remember? Inwardly she shrank from what she was certain would be painful knowledge.

'You will in time.' This was Clive's stock reassurance, but he looked puzzled. Amnesia of recent events was not uncommon after a shock, but not this total blackout. As for her, she found it hard to credit that she had ever known anything else except this primitive house and the wintry landscape around it. Of that she had had a restricted view from her small window, which showed little besides an expanse of glittering frosty whiteness, above a boundary wall, also snow-covered. It was the mountainside that hemmed in the valley, and it reached far above her head. That was on fine days, on others the valley was filled with blankets of grey mist or whirling snowflakes.

Time seemed to stand still during her recovery, marked only by Clive's visits. At first she had regarded him as simply a doctor, an impersonal being whose interest in her was merely that of a medical man in an unusual case, though his touch always thrilled her, but he did not often have occasion to touch her now. In his bulky clothes with his beard and whiskers, he was rather like a youthful Father Christmas, especially as his attitude towards her was always kindly paternal. Since he was the only person with whom she could converse, for she could not understand anything Aziza said, his visits became the high spots of her day. She could not tell him anything about herself beyond what he already knew. It was supposed that she had been with some archaeological expedition, for when Clive showed her some shards of Grecian ware that had been discovered on the site of one of Alexander's cities, they seemed to hold some significance for her. She surmised she must have been on her way to or from some dig. But Clive did not encourage her to think too hard; he feared recollection might inflict a further shock upon her already weakened constitution. Once her bodily health was re-established, her brain would resume its normal functions.

So their conversation was perforce about impersonal matters. He was obsessed by Alexander the Great who had once conquered a vast empire. He waxed enthusiastic about the Macedonian's campaigns, the army of disciplined Greeks who had routed the vastly superior force of the great Persian king, Darius, and chased him to the shores of the Oxus. He made the man come alive for her, although it was some two thousand years since Alexander had been in Afghanistan. It was this great interest of his which had brought him to Nuristan, whose people, legend said, were descended from the Macedonian soldiers, for in the attempt to consolidate his new kingdom, Alexander had encouraged marriages between his men and the natives, setting the example by marrying Roxana, a Bactrian princess. Since the Nuristani had always been isolated in their almost inaccessible mountain fastnesses, the Greek characteristics might well linger, and they were a light-eyed, fair-haired race. Clive thought a stay among them without interference from the outside world might be revealing.

'But you can't dig in the snow,' the girl objected.

'I don't dig, I study people, not ruins.'

'Then have you learned anything about the people here?'

He shrugged his shoulders. 'Not much that wasn't known before. They use chairs,' he pointed to the one in her room. 'Other Eastern people sit on cushions on the floor. Also spoons instead of their fingers. There are archaic Greek words in their language. Once they had a considerable culture, but Abdur Rahman destroyed most of it, on the plea that they were idolators. They declared they were Christians, and maybe their idols were statues of the Virgin and Saints. Anyway, he imposed Islam upon them, and that was that. They still carve wood and live in wooden houses, as you can see.'

He took an object from his pocket and handed it to her. It was a silver disc stamped with a man's head. The girl looked at the straight nose and rounded chin, the sensual mouth and curly hair. It was vaguely familiar.

'A coin from Alexander's day,' Clive told her. 'They're still to be found on the sites of his ruined cities.'

'After all this time?'

'Yes. Afghanistan is a wonderful hunting ground for relics of the past.'

Some fugitive memory flashed through her brain and was gone, suggesting that she had been connected with archaeology.

'He's clean-shaven,' she remarked, studying the coin.

'Most of the younger Greeks were.' He stroked his own impressive growth of beard. 'So am I amid civilised surroundings, but up here it's both convenient and warmer to let it grow.'

She tried to visualise him without his facial hair and failed.

'It makes you look venerable,' she observed.

He smiled wryly. 'Exactly why I get rid of it from time to time. I'm not Methuselah.'

Occasionally, but rarely, he spoke of his personal life. He owned a house and farm in Dorsetshire and had apparently sufficient means to be able to indulge his desire to roam. He never mentioned a wife or fiancée, but apparently he had a mother. Though the girl found his antecedents much more interesting than the history of Alexander, some instinct prevented her from asking questions. Dimly she sensed that some tragedy lay behind his self-imposed exile and he was seeking solace in travel. He told her he wrote books and articles about the countries he visited.

'Are you writing one now?' she enquired.

'I'm making notes, but most of the day I spend with our hosts. As well as attending to their ills, I saw wood for fuel, and help tend the stock. That way I'm learning their language, which is different from the Pushtu and Persian dialects spoken in other parts of the country.'

'I'm afraid you must grudge the time you've spent nursing me,' she said. 'Couldn't you have sent me to a hospital or something?'

He laughed. 'Through twenty-foot snowdrifts? The valley is sealed off now until the spring, and it's not accessible to wheel traffic at any time. I'm glad to have some one of my own race to talk to, for one thing seems indisputable, you're British, and ...' he hesitated, '... you're an interesting case.'

'I'm lucky that you've had some medical experience,' she remarked with slight acidity. She did not wholly relish being labelled as a specimen upon which he could exercise his amateur doctoring. Yet since she owed her life to him she should be grateful. She was grateful, but she wished he would show a little more personal interest in her. He was her only companion, for Aziza hardly counted, but he always kept her at arms' length.

A little reflection showed her she was being unreasonable. Once she was recovered their ways would part, and though of necessity his ministrations were intimate they would become hideously embarrassing if he permitted sex to intrude upon their relationship, for in spite of his venerable beard he was not an old man and she was aware of his magnetic personality.

These conversations always took place in the evenings, for his morning calls were only a brief check-up since he was in a hurry to be about his day's chores, and the girl looked forward to them all day. When evening came, Aziza would settle her in bed, light the inadequate oil lamp, make up the brazier, say something quite incomprehensible with a knowing smirk, and depart.

She did sit up during the day now, in the one chair, but she had nothing to occupy her. All Clive could find for her entertainment was a battered encyclopaedia which he carried with him, and although instructive it was hardly amusing. She was thankful then when bedtime came, and Clive came to her after his evening meal. He would sit on piled cushions on the floor, which he said he preferred to the hard chair, while she lay watching with shadowed eyes the flickering lamplight shine on his golden head and beard so that he looked wholly composed of that metal, the frustrations and boredom of the day forgotten in the pleasure of having him there and listening to the tones of his deep pleasant voice while he talked. Then it was she almost hoped she would never recover her memory, and this happy intercourse could go on for ever. But that was impossible; spring would eventually come to the valley and she would have to leave it ... and him.

Clive taught her a few words of the native language so that she could at least say yes and no to Aziza, but he admitted he was not very proficient in it himself; although he knew several Central Asian languages, Nuristani was unlike any of them.

He called her Angela.

'You must have a name, little waif,' he pointed out, 'and until you can remember your own, it'll serve.'

'But why Angela?'

'Seems appropriate. You dropped from the sky like an angel.'

'I hope it'll prove to be so.' She smiled. 'But angels are not generally depicted with black hair and I don't think my disposition is particularly angelic.'

That reminded her that she knew no more about herself than she did about her past. The garments she had been wearing presented no clue. Trousers and shirt were torn and filthy and bore no recognisable tags. Her luggage and handbag had gone into the abyss with the wreckage of the plane. What sort of a girl was she?, she wondered. Bad or good-tempered? Generous or mean? Friendly or unsociable? Our self-knowledge is built up through the years, but her slate was wiped entirely clean.

She had a great longing to go outside, for her little

room often seemed close and stuffy, and Clive forbade
the window to be opened, in fact it was doubtful if it
would open. The outer air, he declared, was arctic.
That would be preferable to the atmosphere of her
room which always seemed to smell of the mutton fat
the villagers used for cooking, and mutton and kid
were her staple diet, served with rice or flat thin flaps
of unleavened bread. Clive gave her vitamin tablets
from his store of them to make up for the vegetable
deficiency.

One morning when Clive appeared she greeted him
with rebellion.

'I can't endure any more of this room. I'll go mad,
if I'm not mad already! I must get outside. I'm sick to
death of this cell.'

Clive regarded her quizzically.

'You're certainly much better if you feel like that,
though I warn you, I won't stand for mutiny.'

Instantly she changed her tone. 'Then please, Clive,
mayn't I go outside? I am stronger and I don't think it
would hurt me.'

'That's better,' he said with approval.

'Meaning you'll do what I want if I ... grovel?' she
asked with a flash of mischief.

'In this part of the world they consider that the right
attitude for women, and I confess I like to see my
patients properly humble,' he told her arrogantly.

She was tempted to answer back, but decided that
was not the way to get what she wanted, so held her
tongue and Clive went on:

'There's a little sun today, so perhaps a turn in the
open would do you good, if you wrap up.'

He said something to Aziza, who was present, and
she slipped out of the room to return with felt-lined
boots, a sheepskin coat, fur-lined fingerless gloves and

a heavy woollen shawl. This latter item Clive insisted that Angela must wind round her head and face so that only her eyes were visible.

'Aren't I supposed to show my face?' she asked, recalling that Clive had told her this was a Moslem country.

He grinned. 'This isn't the veil, my girl, that's much more comprehensive. The Afghan *chadri* covers you from head to foot, with only a peephole to see where you're going. This is protection against the cold.'

She stumbled going over the threshold, for the floor was uneven and her ankle still weak. With fatherly solicitude he took her arm.

'Lean on me.'

She was glad to do so, and some of his strength seemed to flow into her at the contact.

They entered a second room, connected by a few feet of passage with hers. From the articles strewn about this must be his. A bed similar to her own was along one wall, heaped with spare clothing, maps, and sheets of manuscript, suggesting he was not a tidy person. A typewriter stood upon a carved stool, which looked incongruous in that setting. A beaded curtain, drawn aside from a sort of alcove, revealed a stone slab upon which was an earthenware bowl, and various bottles and packets of medicines.

'Your dispensary?' she asked curiously.

'You could call it that; lucky for you I brought a stock of antibiotics. It was penicillin that saved your life. You had pneumonia, you know.'

But this was no doctor's clinic, only a sideline in his main objective, the study of the people among whom he was living. She had no claim upon him whatever beyond that of common humanity. Impulsively she exclaimed:

19

'What a nuisance I must be to you!'

'I wouldn't say that,' he demurred. 'I've found you quite an interesting psychological study; your reactions to your situation and environment are intriguing.'

'Oh!' She was piqued; in spite of their days of contact, all she was to him was a rare case. 'So you've got me under the microscope as well as Nuristani?' she asked.

The grey eyes glinted.

'Of course.'

About to protest, Angela checked herself as the full impact of her predicament hit her. She was alone among a possibly hostile people and only the fortuitous presence of the man beside her had given her any degree of security. Hitherto, she had taken his ministrations very much for granted, now she began to realise how enormously indebted to him she was. She should be thankful he had found her an interesting case.

The little house was completed by a third room, evidently used for eating, for it contained a table and chairs, and another brazier with a grill for cooking. A Russian samovar stood in one corner, with a row of teapots beside it on a shelf. Green tea was the usual beverage in that country. She took in its details in one quick glance; then Clive opened the outer door, and guided her outside, shutting it quickly behind them to preserve the precious warmth from escaping.

Wrapped up though she was, Angela gasped as the keen wind cut through her thick clothing with the sharpness of a razor blade. They were standing in a village street, with wooden houses huddled all around them, and from a covered corral came the bleating of goats and sheep, but she hardly noticed her immediate surroundings for the awesome beauty of the scene beyond them.

The village lay in a fold of the mountains, above a valley floor which in summer could be tilled, but in winter everything was buried in snow. On the horizon distant peaks like carved white jade rose summit behind summit towards the eastern border. Over all lay a mantle of white glittering in the pale sunlight, except for the deep clefts running back into the mountains which were shadowed with blue and purple, their inmost recesses almost black. The sun was too weak to have any warmth, and the cutting wind spun the surface snow on the valley floor into white froth. Frozen, shining, sunstruck to diamond splendour, it was the enchanted realm of the Snow Queen.

'How beautiful!' she gasped through her muffling shawl. 'But is there any way out?' For the mountains seemed to hem the valley in from every side.

Clive smiled at her naïve question. 'Not in January,' he told her. 'There is a negotiable pass at the end of the valley, but it won't be clear until March.'

'Then I'll be stuck here for another three months?'

'I'm afraid so.'

'And there's no means of communication with anybody?'

'None whatever.'

She was silent, digesting this information. She believed that a return to civilisation would bring her memory back, or if not she could make enquiries to establish her identity, but for many weeks to come she must remain in this limbo with only Clive's company to sustain her. She glanced at him obliquely. His appearance fitted the savage landscape, with his golden beard, the round fur-edged cap on his head, and his sheepskin coat, which she noticed for the first time was embroidered with gold thread, that gleamed in the light of the sun. His keen gaze was raking the valley with the glance of an eagle surveying its territory from its eyrie. She felt small, defenceless and unequal to facing the problems of her future, but so long as she was shut off here alone with him, there would be no problems. But he must resent the isolation that compelled him to continue to offer her refuge.

'You must grudge all the time you have to waste looking after me,' she exclaimed impulsively.

He turned his head to look at her.

'I don't grudge it at all.' A gleam came into the grey eyes. 'There is a certain piquancy about our situation which I find diverting. The villagers believe you're my woman.'

'Oh!' She blushed fierily beneath her shawl, recalling all the intimate services he had performed for her, his room next to hers, with only a few feet of passage between them.

'Why do they think that?' she asked defensively.

'In their world a woman must have a protector. You were dropped by an obliging Allah on the doorstep, so to speak, for my benefit,' he explained lightly. 'So they allocated us a house and provided Aziza to be your handmaiden.'

'I'm glad you find the position amusing,' she told him a little tartly. 'Some people might consider it ambiguous. Have you no ... er ... connections in England who would resent the situation if they got to know about it?'

She watched his face for his reaction eagerly, for this was something she discovered that she very much wanted to know.

He turned away from her, but not before she had seen a shadow fall across his countenance, and again she sensed some hidden tragedy.

'My only female connection is my mother,' he said harshly. 'She's very broad-minded.'

Still trying to probe, she persisted:

'Doesn't she miss you?'

'Possibly, but she likes ruling the roost in my absence,' he told her more gently. 'She's run the place ever since my father died, and doesn't like interference. Of course I go back from time to time to make sure all is well—after all, I'm responsible, and I suppose I'll settle there eventually.' He turned his head to look at her directly. 'As for other ties, men like myself with wandering feet steer clear of matrimony.'

Was there a warning in his steely glance? Angela flushed again, this time with annoyance. Did he imagine she might use their situation to try to trap him? She did not even know if she were free.

'I'm sure you do,' she said icily, 'but in spite of the providence of Allah, you're quite safe from me.'

'I don't regard you as dangerous,' he told her, laughing. 'Poor waif, you're a mere child, and I'm not a cradle-snatcher.'

He dropped a possessive hand upon her shoulder. 'You've been out here long enough, you'll be getting frostbitten,' and turned her back towards the house.

Somewhat unwillingly, Angela re-entered their abode. She wanted—she was not sure what, but she was beginning to find his paternal solicitude irritating.

CHAPTER TWO

As the weeks sped towards spring, Angela became
stronger. Her ankle was perfectly sound again, her
bruises and lacerations had healed without a scar, but
her brain remained clouded. Clive assured her that
sooner or later some incident would cause the veil between her and her past to lift, but he also admitted he
did not know much about mental illness.

'But I'm perfectly sane,' she pointed out.

'Good heavens, girl, I didn't mean you're a nut case,
but I don't understand this blackout. However, when
we reach civilisation again, a specialist will soon put
you right.'

Angela began to view this return with increasing
apprehension, fearing what she might discover.

One day, tentatively handling Clive's portable typewriter, she found she could type. Her fingers remembered a skill that her conscious mind had obliterated.
That solved the problem of filling her empty hours.
Clive gave her his pages of notes to decipher, and not
only was she glad of the occupation, but she was
pleased to feel that she was helping him. Since she
needed no further medical attention, he ceased to
come into her room. Instead they spent the evenings in
the apology for a sitting room, which he made more
habitable by bringing in cushions and rugs from his
bedroom, and installed the typewriter. Then they
would discuss the proposed book, for which her work
was the preliminary, and the country and its ways,
drinking the coffee he brewed on the stove. This came

from his private store; the Nuristani, like the rest of the Afghans, drank tea.

Clothes had been a problem. The shirt and trousers which she had been wearing when found had disintegrated. Aziza produced voluminous skirts, tunics and shawls in which Angela was buried. She was not much of a dressmaker, but she managed to cut them down into something wearable. When she went outside she had the boots and sheepskin coat Clive had procured for her. She had a suspicion that he had paid Aziza in some way for the articles, and thus increased her debt to him. When she tentatively raised the subject, he told her to regard them as payment for her services.

During their evening sessions, he gave her a great deal of information about the country in which she was living, though she would have far rather talked about himself. Realising his deep interest in it and other remote places, she sought to share his enthusiasm. Afghanistan, like many of its neighbours, was changing fast, modernising and developing, with new roads, new schools and buildings, the abolition of the veil and the emergence of women into public life. Politically Russian influence was in the ascendant, the Soviet empire impinging upon the steppes which lay on the further side of the mountains, and only the river Oxus, or Amu Darya, to give it its modern name, dividing the two countries.

But it was the country's history that appealed to Clive, and in which he sought to arouse her interest. Alexander had colonised it, but all the cities he had built had vanished, though Kandahar still bore his name, being a corruption of Iskandar, as he was known in Persian. Genghis Khan had overrun it, bringing slaughter and destruction, and a century later,

Tamerlane. The Hazaras, the people of the central plateau, were descendants of the slit-eyed Mongols and occupied an inferior position to the Pushtuns or Pathans, who were the ruling caste. The races were very mixed and all colourings were to be found there, from blond to brunette, brown, blue, and grey eyes. Kipling had immortalised the Pathans, the proud, arrogant, darkly handsome men who ruled in Kabul. The British had fought three Afghan wars and finally given up trying to subdue the country, confining themselves to guarding the Khyber Pass that connected it with India. Famous, or rather infamous in history, was the terrible massacre of a British Army in retreat from Kabul, the garrison travelling through the snows of winter with its women and children. Every one of them had been wiped out except one man, Doctor Brydon, who had ridden into Jalalabad bearing the dreadful news and there died himself of his wounds.

Clive was also deeply interested in the origins and habits of the nomad population who wandered through the land from the central plateau which they occupied in summer, down to the Indian plains in winter, driving their herds of sheep and goats and loading their gear on to shaggy Bactrian camels. They lived their secret independent lives beholden to no one, and their black pointed tents, guarded by huge, savage dogs, were a feature of many a landscape.

Like Desdemona, Angela listened, and became enthralled while Clive talked, and not only of Afghanistan but the other places he had been in—Greenland, the Sahara, and the forests of Amazonia. And like Desdemona she became more and more fascinated by the hero of these adventures. He was her only companion, for she did not progress with her Nuristani and her communications with Aziza never amounted to con-

26

versation. As for the rest of the villagers, the women always seemed to be indoors when she went out, though they worked in the fields in spring and summer. The men held aloof, quickly averting their eyes if she appeared, even the children seemed to hold her in awe, for they usually ran away if she approached them. This hurt her because she was fond of little ones. When she complained to Clive, he laughed and told her:

'It's because they've been told you're not entirely human and they're afraid you might put a spell upon them. Stories about genies and fairies are common in their folklore, in spite of their conversion to Islam.'

'But couldn't you make them understand I'm just ordinary?'

'You couldn't be to them, my dear; not only was your arrival mysterious, but you live in my house. I'm the great medicine man who has, by the aid of my medicine chest and a little savvy, cured ills they believed incurable. I'm afraid my aura enfolds you as well.'

She remembered he had told her she had been dubbed his woman, and looked at him provocatively, but he merely smiled at her indulgently. He was always kind and friendly, but she doubted if he ever saw her as a woman; she was either a child or an interesting patient. In that connection the dark curtain continued to withhold the knowledge of her identity. Clive told her repeatedly not to worry, one day it would all come back.

Actually she was not worrying at all. She was content to live in this strange white world without past or future, where her whole existence revolved round the personality of Clive Stratton. The future meant separation from him, the past she was convinced held sorrows she wanted to forget. That might account for her persistent blackout. She did not want to remember, nor so long as she remained in her snowbound sanctuary did it matter who she was.

But it had to come to an end. The days lengthened, snow fell less frequently and the icy gales abated. Suddenly it was spring, the snow vanishing from the valley floor and shrinking up the mountainsides. The valley sheltered fruit trees and arable fields, with a river running through them. The goats and sheep ran joyously from rock to rock seeking the hitherto concealed herbage; birds began to sing and the villagers started preparations to plough and sow their fields.

Clive, who had been up to investigate, reported that the pass out of the village was now passable and it was time to start his journey south.

'I'm afraid it will be too arduous a trek for you,' he told Angela, looking at her critically. 'Although you look quite fit now. I propose to leave you here and arrange to send a helicopter to bring you out.'

Angela was appalled; to be left alone with only Aziza whom she could rely upon for an indefinite period was more than she could endure. She pleaded desperately with Clive to be allowed to accompany him. She felt strong enough to face any ordeal, she assured him; she had put on weight and there was now colour in her cheeks. At length he yielded to her pleading, concluding that she was nervous of travelling by air after her experience, and he was a little doubtful if he could procure the services of a helicopter, the only machine which could land in that valley.

'I suppose I must finish the job and get you safe back to civilisation,' he said a little ruefully, 'but it'll be a long, rough journey.'

'Anything would be better than being left alone here,' she insisted, grieved that he showed so little desire for her company. 'But wouldn't you ... I mean ... don't you mind what becomes of me?'

'I'd certainly like to know you're all right and safe with your relations, of which you must have some somewhere. Very well, waif, I won't abandon you.'

And with that she had to be content.

As soon as she understood Angela was going to Kabul, Aziza created an amusing diversion. Although village women went unveiled while working in the fields, when they went to town, they considered their dignity required them to appear in a *chadri*. In vain Clive told her she was old-fashioned, the *chadri* was no longer worn in the capital. The king's household had set an example, appearing in public without covering their faces; Aziza did not believe him. Respectable Moslem women always went veiled and they would always do so.

Some years ago, King Admullah had tried to introduce drastic reforms far too quickly, including the abolition of the veil. This last innovation had cost him his throne. Now it was gradually disappearing and even the Mullahs, the religious leaders, did not object, but Aziza could not or would not accept that it could be so. She produced one of her own *chadris* for Angela's use, and though the girl had no intention of accepting the garment, she could not resist trying it on. Composed of voluminous folds of material, it covered her completely from head to toe, air and vision being admitted through a sort of latticework visor over the face. It seemed to her inconceivable that women had endured its tyranny for centuries whenever they went out.

She went mincing into Clive's room to show herself,

though there was nothing to see of her except her feet.

'At least it wouldn't matter how old or ugly one was,' she remarked. 'It hides everything.'

He laughed. 'Afghan men declare they always knew if a veiled woman was young and pretty; a sort of sixth sense, I suppose. Incidentally, a woman always walked one pace behind her man, less I fancy as a sign of inferiority than for protection. Still, she did serve her husband on bended knee and address him as Presence. Now all that is going, women have the vote and are being encouraged to go out to work.' His eyes gleamed mischievously. 'Such a pity! I would like to possess a subservient wife and have the exclusive right to view her face.'

'For shame,' Angela rebuked him, laughing. 'You're a westerner, Clive, not an Eastern despot.'

'But you must admit a veil is very intriguing.' He touched the long folds. 'Imagine the excitement of drawing it aside to discover what's underneath!'

'And finding a plain jane, which would serve you right.' There was an unfamiliar glint in his eyes which made her feel a little breathless. 'If you want to play the Eastern potentate, you'd look more in character if you wore a turban.'

'I rate a *karaculi*, not a turban, as I rank as a *khan*, and I believe you've seen me in one.'

He was referring to the karacul hat which was the common wear of city men.

'It's not nearly so impressive as a turban. I suggest a pink one with a tail such as Aziza's son swaggers around in.'

'Wouldn't suit my colouring—and don't you go making eyes at young Abdullah, it might give him ideas.'

'Not him, he always looks the other way when he sees me.'

Clive looked up at her teasingly from the pile of cushions upon which he was sprawled upon the floor. He was wearing a knitted sweater, which appeared a little incongruous with his boots and baggy trousers.

'Doesn't want to poach upon my preserves, and that get-up of yours is giving *me* ideas. It rouses the dominating male in me. By rights you should be kneeling before me.'

Angela felt a faint stir of excitement; she had not met this mood in him before. She said decisively:

'I'm not going to pander to you, and from what you've told me, Afghan women are absorbing Western ideas about sex equality.'

'More's the pity,' he said shortly.

'You believe in keeping women subservient?'

He smiled wryly. 'It makes life easier for the men, but it will be a long time before Western notions really get a hold. An unfaithful wife is still regarded as an outcast and her brothers and father are quite capable of putting her to death to wipe out the shame she's brought upon the family.'

'How dreadful!'

He shrugged his shoulders. 'Afghan men can be devils when their passions are aroused, and they have their own peculiar idea of honour.'

'I don't suppose they're always faithful.'

'That's different.'

'The double standard?'

His eyes glinted sardonically. 'Dear me, waif, you've got the jargon off pat, haven't you? Perhaps you were an ardent supporter of women's rights in your forgotten past, but I hope not.'

'I'm all for fairness and justice,' she said earnestly.

'My child, you rarely get either between men and women—emotionalism blinds them.'

31

His eyes went beyond her and his face became bleak as a winter's day. 'Women are the unfair sex in that respect,' he stated. 'A taste of good old oriental discipline would do some I've known a lot of good. Sluts who enjoy playing havoc with men's tenderest feelings, and expect to get away unscathed.'

He spoke more to himself than to her, and she thought he had forgotten her presence lost in some painful memory. She slipped off the shrouding garment and folded it carefully. There must have been women in his life; he was too virile a man to be indifferent to sex, even her innocence realised that. One must have played him false, and that was why he wandered over the earth seeking for forgetfulness. She was a little shocked by his vindictive tone. Even if he had been let down, he was not an Afghan, and such a naturally kindly man must surely take a more charitable view of feminine frailty. She said tentatively:

'But you can't believe an incompatible couple should remain bound together in mutual unhappiness?'

His eyes came back to her as if her voice had recalled him from a long distance.

'Were we discussing incompatible couples?' he asked mildly. 'I thought it was the Afghan attitude towards infidelity. Only a few years ago they stoned unfaithful wives in the Biblical manner.'

'Ugh!' She shivered. 'How inhuman! You can't condone that.'

Clive grinned. 'Perhaps that was going a little too far, but no doubt it was an effective deterrent. Psychological disturbances didn't get any sympathy in the seraglio, and I don't know that our new freedoms have made women—or men either—any happier.'

The sombre look returned to his face, and he sprang

to his feet, scattering the cushions as he took a quick pace across the room, saying savagely:

'The more I see of women, the more convinced I am that the right way to treat them is to keep them shut up in a harem.'

Angela stared at him in astonishment, voice and demeanour were so at variance with his usual pleasant manner. His beard actually seemed to bristle with suppressed anger, and he clenched and unclenched his hands. Someone at some time must have wounded him very deeply, and she felt a surge of indignation against that unknown woman, whose mere memory could so shake his normal tolerance.

She said uncertainly:

'That sounds a bit drastic, what have we poor women done to merit such animosity?'

He turned and stared at her as if surprised to find her still there.

'Present company excepted, of course,' he told her awkwardly. He passed his hand over his brow and smiled apologetically. 'I suppose it was that,' he pointed to the *chadri*, 'that touched me off, that and ... er ... other things. Forget it.' He looked at her consideringly. 'You're still only a child in experience.'

'That we don't know,' she reminded him.

'It's obvious,' he insisted, 'I haven't lived with you all these weeks without learning that. You haven't yet acquired the damnable wiles of a sophisticated woman.'

A little nettled, for he was suggesting that she was naïve, she cried with spirit:

'And do you know so much about sophisticated women? I thought you were only familiar with primitive peoples.'

'I've lived in cities,' he informed her drily, 'the only

difference being that among primitive people I've seen the material in the raw. The basic instincts are the same.' With indescribable bitterness in his voice, he added: 'When Miss Afghanistan realises her potentialities, her menfolk will regret letting her out of purdah.'

'Well, you've got me in a sort of purdah here,' Angela remarked, 'since even Abdullah daren't look at me.'

He laughed, and lightly flipped her cheek with his fingertip.

'True woman, aren't you?' She didn't think he meant it as a compliment. 'But at least I've kept you out of harm's way for whoever is waiting for you.'

Angela picked up the *chadri* in silence. Was someone waiting for her? Fervently she hoped not. She smoothed the long folds over her arm; her innocent desire to try the garment on seemed to have provoked Clive's tirade against her sex, which was far from her intent. He looked at her bent dark head with a curious expression. She seemed very young, very vulnerable and quite incapable of the wiles against which he had been inveigling.

'You'd better return that thing to Aziza as tactfully as possible,' he said laconically. Suddenly he seemed to relax and a twinkle came into his eye. 'Unless you want to wear it on our trek and walk respectfully one pace behind me.'

'Certainly not.' She moved to the door and said over her shoulder: 'That wouldn't be suitable since I'm not your wife.'

His face darkened. 'No, you're not that,' he said emphatically.

Angela went through into her own room, reflecting that she had asked for it, and there was no doubt from Clive's look and tone that he was thankful there was

34

no emotional attachment between them. The knowledge was a little wounding, for she was not without feminine conceit, but she comforted her ego by deciding he would be a very uncomfortable sort of husband if he expected complete submission from his wife. Perhaps that was what had broken up his romance, for she was certain now that there had been one. Clive Stratton was too despotic to appreciate the modern girl's independent outlook. Yet he must have cared deeply if her memory kept him roaming over the waste places of the globe. Angela felt a burning curiosity about that woman who had left such a cruel scar, but knew she could not possibly question Clive to satisfy it. In fact her own association with him was nearing its end, and that thought produced a deep depression.

Though Clive was capable of accomplishing the arduous journey on foot, he was unwilling to allow Angela to essay it. They would find buses, he told her, once they had climbed out of the valley and crossed the pass, but their routes were many miles away. She must ride. He went from village to village in search of mules and eventually procured a pair of scrawny animals, which he brought home in triumph. One would carry Angela, the other his gear.

This transaction caused her some perturbation. As far as she knew she possessed nothing, and she was being an ever-increasing expense to her benefactor. Even when they reached civilisation she would still be dependent upon his bounty. When she hesitantly hinted at her poverty, he pooh-poohed her scruples.

'I had to get one mule anyway, I couldn't lug the typewriter all the way, and I got the two cheap, and I must owe you quite a lot for all that typing you've done for me, far more than the few *afghanis* I've given Aziza for clothes,' he told her. 'You can continue to be my secretary in Kabul until a more satisfactory arrangement can be made for you.' He surveyed her thoughtfully. 'I'm sure once we're there we'll be able to trace your relatives through the air company's records. At least they must have a list of the missing passengers, and one of the names will surely ring a bell.'

She clasped her hands nervously, dreading that moment of revelation. The past months had been a period of suspension between her past and her future, and she shrank from what those records might tell her. Clive saw the tension in her face and laid a comforting hand over hers.

'Come now, you can't want to exist for ever in limbo.'

She could not voice the fear that was uppermost in her mind. Suppose she discovered that she belonged to another man? Clive had become her whole world, friend, doctor, and protector. By nature something of a leaner, he was her bulwark against life's problems. She could not contemplate an existence without him to support her. But he naturally would be wanting to be rid of her, she must have been an imposition in spite of his denials. She consoled herself with that vague suggestion that she might continue as his secretary. It was her anchor in a sea of uncertainties.

It was a bright cloudless day when they set off, Clive told Angela it was only a respite before rainy weather would set in, the rain that was necessary to make the crops grow. The path, if path it could be called, snaked up a boulder-strewn route out of the valley. Looking back, Angela saw the wooden houses of the village clinging to the cliff ledge upon which they were built like a group of swallows' nests, and reflected that she had in fact been happy during her sojourn there, a happiness that was largely due to Clive's company. He walked ahead of her leading the other mule, whistling gaily. He had no regrets, though neither of them would see that village again.

The pass was a narrow passage between towering cliffs, where since the sun never penetrated its shadows, snow still lingered. Beyond it the barely discernible track crept along the edge of fearsome abysses and under beetling overhangs of bare rock. Occasionally it widened into stone-strewn plateaus where a scant herbage struggled for existence. The melting snow cascaded down the mountainsides in waterfalls that often crossed their route and through which they had to pass. The sure-footed mules seemed unperturbed by the difficulties of the road, and Angela's thick sheepskin coat and boots kept out most of the wet. They halted at midday for food and rest on a broad ledge above a shadow-filled ravine. The mountains all around them were bare and stark, not at all Alpine in character, the lower ones looking more like giant gnarled mounds of earth instead of peaks.

Clive hobbled the mules and left them to crop eagerly at the coarse grass. He had filled a thermos with welcome coffee before leaving, and produced kebabs, grilled on the brazier in their hut, and a flap of the usual barley bread.

'We should make a village where I'm known before nightfall,' he told her, 'and the road tomorrow will be much less gruelling.'

'That's something,' she laughed a little shakily, for she had found their awesome surroundings intimidating. 'But will your villagers welcome me?'

'Of course, you're my woman,' he gave her a mischievous glance. 'And whatever other failings they have, Afghans never lack in hospitality. A guest is sacred, and a poor man will share his last tea-leaf with one.'

They reached the village in the late afternoon. It was encircled by high mud walls and looked like a miniature fortress, but there was no doubt about their welcome. A flock of brown-skinned, black-haired children raced into the adobe huts to give notice of their arrival, and the headman came out himself to greet them, embracing Clive like a long-lost brother.

They had descended several thousand feet and the air was almost balmy, fruit trees were coming into blossom outside the village walls, and there was fresh grass for the mules. On a fire in the middle of the compound, a lamb was put to roast in their honour. Angela stood a little apart while Clive unpacked their gear. Instinctively she had drawn her scarf across the lower part of her face, more from shyness than from modesty, aware of the curious glances thrown in her direction. Giving their luggage to the willing porterage of the older children, Clive came across to her.

'I'm afraid we can't expect a hut to ourselves,' he told her, 'and I've been invited to join the men for a feast. You'll be accommodated in the women's quarters in the head man's house. They'll look after you, so you needn't be afraid.'

'Can't I stay with you?' she asked anxiously, dreading to be separated from him.

'Impossible, dinner is strictly for men only. You'll be all right, Angela, no need to panic.'

So perforce she had to leave him and enter the women's quarters. The headman's family consisted of wives, mothers, grandmothers, and daughters of all ages—impossible to sort them out. They welcomed her with smiles and obvious curiosity, bringing her water to wash her hands and face, but they could only con-

verse by signs. Bone weary as she was they seemed to
Angela like fantastic figures in a dream. They gave her
green tea to drink and fresh mutton with rice to eat.
All, she noticed, wore quantities of jewellery, even the
little girls. It represented their savings.

Finally she was shown a mat in a corner covered
with several skins and thick quilts, and so weary was
she that she fell asleep immediately, in spite of the
noise from the compound, where the men were evidently enjoying themselves.

On the evening of the next day they reached a much
larger village and one that possessed a caravanserai, or
tea-house. This one, Clive told her, was on a bus route,
and they would have transport for the rest of their
journey.

As they neared it, Clive pulled a silk shawl from his
baggage and handed it to her.

'Keep that over your face,' he commanded her,
'you'll find it less stifling than the woollen scarf you
wore last night.'

'But must I wear one at all? I thought you said the
veil was obsolete.'

'In Kabul, but emancipation mayn't have reached as
far as this.' He glanced at her legs. She wore a tunic
and a pair of men's breeches above her boots. 'Have
you got a skirt among your things?'

'Look,' she began forcibly, 'this gear was your idea,
though it shocked Aziza, since I was going to ride, but
I won't be bundled up into any more clothes to suit
your belated sense of propriety. I'm hot enough as it
is.'

'All right, you can change at the inn. But keep your
face covered.'

Obediently she wrapped the silk around her head
and face, leaving only her eyes exposed. Thus muffled

39

she rode up to the tea-house. The space in front of it was full of men, bold wild-looking hillmen with knives stuck in their belts and dark eyes flashing under their turbans. They carried themselves with the arrogant pride that is characteristic of their race, and Angela guessed they were Pushtuns, or Pathans as they are sometimes called. She saw them throw furtive glances in her direction and Clive assumed a fierce scowl, as befitted a jealous husband when other men glanced at his wife. She had to stifle a desire to giggle, it was so absurd, but she realised it was assumed for her protection. The serai was a long, low building and looked dirty and neglected, but evidently it was familiar ground to Clive, for he called loudly:

'Shere Shah!'

A pink-turbaned individual with the countenance of a brigand in a melodrama came hurrying out of the building. Seeing Clive, he bowed ceremoniously and began a flow of compliments and enquiries. Clive cut him short with a demand for a room for the Khanum Sahib. The man shot a startled look at Angela and his manner changed completely. He stood with bowed head and folded hands while Clive helped Angela to dismount. Throwing the reins of the two animals to a lively-looking Hazara lad who appeared to be a member of the staff, Clive took Angela's arm and piloted her in the wake of the innkeeper. They went through a room of which the walls were painted with red frescoes of rifles and daggers, in the centre of which an iron stove was roaring, exuding an aroma of resinous pine wood. Angela halted, liking the warmth and colour of it, but Clive propelled her forward, for there were men seated on benches all round the walls. The upper room—it was only a loft—that she finally entered after climbing a ladder-like stair, was a small rectangular box with a square of window high up on the wall containing a string bedstead.

'Hardly the Ritz,' Clive commented, surveying it, 'but it's the best they can offer, and at least it's private.'

'The room downstairs was much pleasanter.'

'You can't expect them to evacuate it for a mere woman,' he said mockingly. 'Tea-houses are still a masculine preserve. However, I daresay we can improve this one.'

The Hazara boy brought a brazier and an oil lamp, keeping his eyes discreetly downcast in front of Angela. Some cushions were produced which Angela eyed dubiously before seating herself upon them, they did not look very clean. Clive went to fetch their supper, and returned with eggs fried in mutton fat, which was all the place could provide, and of course a pot of tea. He unearthed spoons from their baggage, the natives ate with their fingers. They sat side by side on the bed to eat their meal.

Uneasily listening to the shouts and singing from below and what sounded like a quarrel, Angela enquired anxiously:

'I suppose this is where I'm to sleep, if I can, but where will you be, Clive?'

'With my wife, of course,' he returned with a sly glance at her, 'that will be expected of me.'

'Do you have to tell them all I'm your wife?'

'What else? They wouldn't understand our ... er ... peculiar relationship.'

She glanced round the small room which he seemed to fill and felt herself blush.

'There isn't much space,' she faltered.

'Nor any toilet facilities,' he pointed out. 'You'll have to go to bed unwashed—as for other things, there's the great out of doors.'

'With all those men about?'

'I will keep guard.'

The intimacy of their situation caused her to blush anew. Yet she had spent two whole days with him in easy camaraderie, and weeks of solitude in the village. It was the single small room and the bed that had suddenly made their association significant.

'It's ... it's only like camping out,' she said bravely.

'Of course.'

He did not seem in the least embarrassed, but then he never had regarded her as a woman, only as a patient, or a child, and certainly not as a wife.

The boy brought in their baggage, and Clive insisted that she unpacked a skirt for the morrow's wear. She had brought with her some of the crude garments she had made over from Aziza's.

'I shall look a sketch,' she sighed. 'A tacky old skirt and that shawl over my head.'

'To travel on the bus you must look like a modest Moslem wife, since you've no European clothes,' he pointed out.

'Then I'll match you, for you look anything but civilised,' she retorted, glancing at his length of hair and beard, and hillman's dress.

'That's the whole idea,' he returned gravely.

She slept indifferently on the string bed, but Clive lay outside her door, wrapped in a blanket.

CHAPTER THREE

ANGELA woke early to a bright clear dawn. Somewhere outside a cock was crowing, but there was no other sound; the noisy visitors of the previous night had either gone or were still asleep. She was stiff and aching from the previous two days of travel and she longed for a hot bath, but that of course was out of the question. She was still wearing most of her clothes and she had used her coat to cover her. Remembering Clive's injunction about a skirt, she got up and changed her trousers for one of those which she had worn in the village. It was of dark patterned material and was both long and full. Over it she put on the tunic blouse with wide sleeves, which she had worn with the trousers, but not her coat, which was too thick and heavy for her present milder environment. She brushed and re-plaited her hair and wound the shawl that Clive had produced about her head and face. It was of black silk and similar to those of coarser material which the village women wore. She wondered if he had brought it for the purpose of disguising her. A modest Moslem wife! If that meant covering everything up, she looked the part, but how far from the truth. If only she were in reality Clive's wife the future would hold no terrors for her, but once they had arrived in Kabul, she would have to fend for herself, and she felt quite incapable of doing so.

There was no sign of Clive when she opened her door and she felt a pang of contrition as she looked down at the bare boards. How uncomfortable he must have been during the night, and he could have found better accommodation downstairs, but he had stayed beside her door like a faithful watchdog so that no one could disturb her without waking him. A warm rush of gratitude welled up in her. How could she ever repay him for his care of her?

She climbed down the rickety stair and found to her relief that the room below was empty, and the door ajar. A shaft of gold from the new-risen sun spilled through it on the dusty floor. Hoping to find a well or a pump where she could at least wash her face and hands, Angela went outside. Here for a moment she forgot her discomfort as she gazed at the awe-inspiring scene. Mountains on either hand rose in majestic grandeur, those on the trail they had come down the day before receding further and further back to ranges of still higher peaks until they became lost in cloud.

She did not see a well, but her quick ears caught the sound of running water. She ran recklessly in its direction until she came upon a mountain torrent swollen by melting snow, and foaming over the boulders in its path. She walked beside it looking for an accessible place where she could reach it, and eventually came upon a flat ledge of rock overhanging a limpid pool. Kneeling down, she stripped off veil and blouse, careless of unseen watchers, and laved her arms and neck in the icy water. It was refreshing and invigorating. Feeling much better, she dried herself with the shawl, and resumed her blouse. Letting the shawl float behind her on the breeze, she made her way back, hoping it would soon dry.

She had come further than she had thought, and before she could reach the inn, she was met by a scowling Clive coming towards her.

'Where the devil have you been?' he demanded. 'I

was half out of my mind wondering where you could have got to.'

'I only went to find a place where I could perform my toilet,' she said meekly. 'And you seemed to have disappeared. Were you afraid one of your villainous-looking cronies had abducted me? I wouldn't put it past them.'

'Nor would I,' he returned, 'you look quite appetising in spite of those ill-fitting clothes.'

'Thank you, kind sir, my ego needs a boost, I feel as if I'd come out of a rag bag. But where have you been?'

'Disposing of the mules. We shan't need them any more. And I made a profit on them.'

'Do buses really come up here?' she asked, looking at the rough road.

'Oh, yes, they manage even worse terrains than this, but their timetable is a bit elastic. Meanwhile the boy is taking breakfast up to our room, so you'd better come and have it. And put that thing back round your face.'

'Why? There's no one about, and it's damp.'

'Do as I say. You're probably being watched from behind every crag.'

'Does it matter?'

'Yes. And while you're with me, you'll obey me.'

He looked so menacing that she dared not argue further, but put the shawl over her head, leaving her face uncovered. He stepped up to her, gathered the two ends in each hand, and drew it over her mouth and chin, knotting it behind her head.

'Contumacious,' he growled.

Effectively gagged, she gave him a defiant look, out of narrowed dark eyes, and with a short laugh, he took her by the arm and propelled her towards the inn.

'You don't know what's good for you,' he told her, 'but I do.'

She had to admit he had a point, for when they reached the tea-house, a camel train had just arrived, and Angela had to run the gauntlet of insolent dark eyes, as Clive bundled her back inside and up to their stuffy little room.

'The glamour of being an eastern houri is much exaggerated,' she said, as she pulled off her drapery. 'You nearly suffocated me.'

'Never mind, I'll make it up to you when we reach Kabul,' he told her kindly. 'But I don't want you to arouse any interest at this stage. You've neither a travel permit nor a passport, and we may just get by by preserving the wifely fiction.'

'I'm sorry,' she was contrite. Then with a flash of spirit. 'If you were really my husband, I wouldn't let you bully me.'

'Nor would I let you defy me,' he returned. 'But since I'm not ...' He shrugged his shoulders. 'Let's have breakfast.'

There was only bread and raisins to eat with the ubiquitous tea. Clive said it was a pity it was too early for melons, which were a great feature of Afghan diet. They boasted that they grew the finest melons and grapes in the world.

Since the camel drivers were occupying the tea-house, Clive would not permit her to go out again, and she had to remain in the bedroom until the bus arrived, while he mingled with the men downstairs, drinking tea with them and swopping adventure stories. Angela fumed alone upstairs, and reflected that she was gaining a very good idea of what it was like to be in purdah, and emancipation was spreading far too slowly. Clive might at least have kept her company,

46

but perhaps he was punishing her for going out without permission in the early morning. A nasty, vengeful character, Clive Stratton, and she was thankful she was not really his wife. But she was deceiving herself. She might try to whip up indignation against him, but in her heart of hearts she would have been thankful to be Mrs Clive Stratton.

Eventually the bus came. It was an unwieldy-looking vehicle painted a bright blue with flower patterns in its panels. The driver also had a bunch of flowers in his cab. Afghans loved flowers and it was not unusual to see a fierce-looking Pushtun with a rose behind his ear, or carried carefully in his fingers. The bus was divided into three portions, first-class next the driver, the centre divided by partitions was for ladies, and the rear section was for men. Angela, to her great disgust, was confined in the ladies only, while Clive sat with the driver. Their baggage was piled on the roof. Angela had only one companion, a country woman shrouded in a *chadri*. Remembering what Clive had said, and suspecting the dimly seen eyes were contemptuous, Angela felt almost naked, as she sat opposite to her on the narrow seat. At home, the woman would have gone unveiled, for such drapery would hinder her work in the fields, but when she went to town she defied the new emancipation by wearing it. Idiot, Angela thought scornfully, pulling her shawl closer round her face, she doesn't know what's good for her—and remembered Clive had told her the same thing. But were Eastern women so foolish? Weren't they seeking to preserve an air of mystery which Western women had entirely lost? Conversation being impossible Angela smiled ingratiatingly at her companion hoping to lessen her antagonism. This proved to be entirely illusionary, for the woman produced from under her copious drapery a bag containing a sticky sort of nougat, which she offered to Angela. Sensing a refusal would be hurtful, Angela accepted doubtfully and bravely ate it, nodding her thanks. A further irritation was that the glass in the bus windows was tinted blue, thus obscuring the view of the passing countryside, which still seemed to be mountains, though the road was rapidly losing height. The veiled woman snored gently, and Angela realised she was asleep. Finally despite the jolting, and because she had passed a bad night, Angela also dozed.

It seemed an interminable journey. At noon the bus stopped, and peering out, Angela saw the more devout of the passengers had descended into the roadway to say their prayers. Her companion made no move, though she turned slightly in her seat and bowed her head. Later they stopped for refreshment at what appeared to be a small town, and which was apparently the woman's destination. She was joined by a turbaned ruffian from the back of the vehicle and Angela was surprised by the tender smile with which he greeted his wife. They walked away, the woman keeping the prescribed pace behind her husband. Angela lost no time in getting out herself. She found the air was much milder than higher in the mountains, and the fields on either side of the road were covered with scarlet tulips, a small variety with pointed petals.

'You should have stayed on the bus,' Clive said as he joined her.

'Oh, but I must stretch my legs,' she protested, 'and it's high time emancipation was extended to public vehicles.'

'Country places are always reactionary,' he remarked, 'but don't British Rail have ladies only compartments?'

'If they still do I never travel in them.'

'How do you know?'

She flushed and stammered. She did not know, nor could she recall anything about the facilities of British Rail. But presumably she must have travelled upon trains, if she lived in Britain. She did not even know that.

'Never mind, come and eat,' Clive bade her.

They sat together by the roadside eating bread and goat's cheese, washed down with coffee, for Clive had replenished his thermos at the caravanserai. The blue of the sky was becoming overcast and a fine rain was falling as they hastily sought the shelter of the bus. The vehicle proceeded on its way, but now several women had invaded Angela's compartment, one with a baby which she proceeded to nurse. Angela conceded then that segregation did have its advantages.

Before and after sunset, the bus again halted for what Angela designated as the prayer meeting. In spite of the drizzling rain the devout ones clambered out to kneel on the mats they carried with them. Then darkness fell and for what seemed interminable hours, Angela dozed and woke and dozed again as the bus bumped and rocked on its downward journey. She felt she had been travelling thus for ever.

At long last they rattled into Kabul.

'You'll have forgotten what civilisation is like,' Clive remarked, as they changed into a *ghari*, one of the one-horse carriages that still plied for hire in the city streets in competition with the taxis.

She said soberly: 'That's one of the things I've got to remember, if I can.'

He had spoken without thinking, but what he had said was only too true. She had forgotten.

As they drove to the hotel, Angela peered out eagerly

at the city, wondering if it would seem familiar. The streets were asphalt and there seemed to be roads lined with mud brick villas among trees, rows of dusty shops, conglomerations of buses, *gharis*, and donkeys. Then they came to a modern avenue lit by lamps, where there were four-storey government buildings and the new hotel. Angela sighed, everything looked new and strange.

At the Hotel Kabul, the best in the town, Clive dismissed the *ghari*. Laden with their cumbersome baggage, he signed to Angela to follow him into the foyer. This was vast and furnished with a wealth of Italian furniture. Fluorescent lamps poured a flood of light down upon an inch-thick carpet and rows of vacant chairs.

There were several people standing about who looked like European tourists. They stared curiously at the big golden-bearded man, who looked as though he had tramped in from the back of beyond, as indeed he had. Angela, following timidly in his wake, felt acutely conscious of her clumsy clothing and boots which were so out of place among so much grandeur.

Clive stalked imperturbably up to the long reception desk, where a clerk in an impeccable European suit was presiding, and dumped his luggage at its foot.

Some sort of argument seemed to ensue as he handed over his passport, and Angela remembered uneasily that she did not possess one, which she supposed was an offence; but Clive would find a way round it, she thought confidently, he could think up a solution for every difficulty. Apparently he had done so, for the desk clerk was smiling amicably after a bundle of *afghani* notes had changed hands. A porter in a white tunic appeared and picked up their bundles, and Clive turned to her with an odd smile. Drawing her a little to one side, he told her in a low voice:

'I'm afraid we'll have to continue with the masquerade for a little longer. I've only been able to get you in here by declaring you're my wife, and so new that your name hasn't yet been added to my passport. I've registered you as Mrs Stratton. I don't know if our friend believed me.' He nodded towards the clerk, who was watching them with a knowing eye. 'But I promised that tomorrow we'll be going to the police, as of course we shall, to straighten out your position, but meanwhile,' he gave her a quizzical glance, 'we've been given a double room.'

'We'll manage somehow,' she said, ignoring the implication behind his words. After all they had shared restricted accommodation before, and she trusted Clive entirely, but her heart sank for another reason. Would she be able to establish her identity on the morrow, and if she could not, what was to become of her? She could not continue to trade upon Clive's generosity, borrowing even his name. Mrs Stratton ... Angela Stratton, and she had no claim to either. She was Miss Nobody from nowhere until the block in her memory was removed.

Another white-coated porter was waiting to conduct them to their room, and as soon as they reached it, a third appeared, carrying tea in a big flower-patterned tea-pot, which he put on a table in front of the window. Then he bowed and with an obsequious smirk retired.

'Isn't it terribly expensive?' Angela asked, overawed by all this service and the big well furnished room.

'I can afford it,' Clive told her, laughing at her anxious expression. 'I haven't had any chance to spend money this winter, and after that trek I think we deserve a little luxury.'

The room promised to supply that. Twin beds were inconspicuous at one end of it, with bedside lamps beside them. There were built-in wardrobes and modern dressers. Two armchairs were set in the window on either side of the table, and a chaise-longue stood against one wall. The floor was covered with fitted thick piled carpet and there was a profusion of cushions.

'Who stays here?' she enquired, thinking the hotel was out of keeping with Afghanistan's alleged poverty.

'Tourists and oil sheikhs, I imagine.' Clive was pouring out the tea.

While she drank it, Angela continued to study her surroundings. She knew that she had been in a similar room before. Hitherto her environment had been completely novel with nothing to touch a chord of memory; even the town had seemed strange, but this was familiar, though on a grand scale. Hotel bedrooms bear a certain similarity the world over, but where had she stayed in one, and with whom?

While she pondered, Clive, having finished his tea, was investigating the bathroom. She heard the sound of running water. Standing in the open door of it, he told her:

'The water is actually hot, and I'm running a bath for you. You'll find it a great improvement on that stream this morning.'

'But you?'

He gave her a mock bow. 'Ladies first.'

She needed no further invitation, but seizing her bag, scurried into the bathroom. White enamel and shining chromium fittings were also familiar, but she wasted no time in cogitation. Stripping off her clothes, she stepped into the steaming water, and enjoyed the first real bath in months.

There were large Turkish towels provided, and wrapped in one of them, after completing her ablutions, she surveyed her peculiar assortment of clothing provided by Aziza with distaste, wishing she had something fresh to put on. Sighing, she resumed the coarse chemise and petticoat, her skirt and blouse, and walking barefoot—she had no slippers or shoes—carried her boots and bag back into the bedroom.

'It's all yours, Clive.'

While he in his turn bathed, she sat down on the chaise-longue and undid the plaits which she had tied up on top of her head, brushing out the long silky strands. It fell about her like a shining ebony cloak.

Clive came out of the bathroom, arrayed in an embroidered shirt and baggy pants, also a pair of Arabian slippers he had carried in his baggage. His beard and hair sparkled with moisture. He stood looking at the slight girlish figure on the chaise-longue swathed in her long tresses, and looking up, Angela caught a glint in his grey eyes, and for a long moment their gaze locked. She felt her pulse begin to race, and her colour rose under that intent regard. Clive was seeing her as a woman, and possibly a desirable one, but all he said was:

'Your hair's grown quite a lot since you were ill.'

'It has, hasn't it?' She tried to speak casually.

He turned away. 'Put it up, child. It's too ... er ... distracting for our present situation.'

Disappointed, she began to plait it, but what had she expected? A declaration of some sort? A display of emotion? Clive had himself too well in hand to do either, even if he were attracted, and she dared hardly hope he was.

'We look a nice pair of ragamuffins amidst all this grandeur,' she observed. 'We can't go down to dinner

53

looking as we do.'

Dinner? That was what one ate at a hotel. Again memory had stirred.

'I'll have some food brought up to us,' he said absently, and moving to the dressing table began to brush his yellow mane. 'This'll have to be cut tomorrow, I look like a hippy.'

'Surely there aren't any in Afghanistan?' She spoke at random, her feminine intuition aware of an undercurrent.

'They come through in shoals on their way to India, and batten on the native hospitality. We don't want to be mistaken for drop-outs.' Though he had his back to her, she suspected he was watching her in the mirror. She finished her second braid, and glancing up under her eyelashes, enquired:

'What can we do about it?'

'What? Oh, yes.' He took a grip upon himself and turned from the mirror with a businesslike air. 'We'll have to get you something to wear before we present ourselves to the police. What's your size?'

She told him, and stared at him in surprise. 'I ... I remembered.'

'So you did. But perhaps you've grown a bit. We'll make sure.'

With the aid of a ruler and a piece of string, neither carried a tape measure, he made her measure her hips, waist and bust, carefully noting the inches on a piece of the hotel writing paper.

'But can't I go into a shop and try something on?' she asked.

'You're not going outside in daylight until you're properly dressed. I'll have something sent in.'

She cried distressfully: 'However am I going to repay you for ... for everything?'

'Now don't start worrying about that,' he said firmly. 'You've quite enough on your plate without considering finance. We'll probably find you've got means of your own, once we've established your identity.'

'If I have, I'll repay you every penny,' she declared earnestly. 'But money can't repay all your care for me. I'll be eternally in your debt.'

'What a burden for a poor waif to bear,' he said mockingly. 'Perhaps I can suggest a way to ease it.'

Again there was a gleam in his eyes, and she stared back at him wonderingly. Could he possibly mean ...?

He turned away abruptly. 'I too need a change of gear. I left some clothes here to be collected upon my return, but I'll not bother to get them tonight.' He yawned. 'I'm too damn tired.'

Angela glanced towards the twin beds. 'I hope ...' she began, and stopped. She was remembering how last night he had slept, or tried to do so, outside her door. Would he feel it was necessary to do that again? But he could not sleep in the hotel corridor.

'We have a good night,' he finished for her. 'I'm sure we shall!' He threw her an enigmatical glance.

A meal was brought up to them by a slit-eyed waiter, who glanced at Angela surreptitiously, evidently wondering what the fine, bearded Sahib could find desirous in such a skinny wife. After it had been removed, Clive yawned again and stretched.

'Shall we waive the proprieties and sample those beds?' he asked. 'Or will that offend your maiden modesty?'

With heightened colour she said, 'I don't see what else we can do.'

'I might sleep in the bath.'

'Oh, don't be so absurd, Clive. You'd be very uncom-

55

fortable. After all, it isn't like ... a double bed.'

'Just so,' he drawled. 'And I don't think I snore.' He pushed the beds further apart. 'Pity there isn't a screen.'

'I look quite nice in bed,' she told him pertly.

'Too nice,' he returned. 'I've seen you.'

'Of course, when I was your patient. You're half a doctor, so you're used to seeing women in bed.' She strove to speak lightly, to break the tension which seemed to be developing.

'With one exception my patients didn't have beds, and I never slept with them.' His eyes glinted wickedly.

Suddenly alarmed, Angela stammered: 'You won't ... you aren't ... I mean ...'

He gave her a long look and laughed. 'Rest easy, Angela, it's only your reputation that's in jeopardy, and we'll deal with that problem if and when it arises. Suppose you get to bed, Mrs Stratton, and I'll take a turn outside while you undress. By the time I come back, you'll be sound asleep.'

She was not, but she pretended to be when he returned, so noiselessly that she only knew he was there when she saw his shadow on the wall, cast by the shaded light from the bedside lamp. He went into the bathroom and returned in only his shirt. She heard the other bed creak as he lay down upon it, and darkness descended as he switched off the light. She heard him give a deep sigh of content, and then silence.

Angela could not sleep, she was overtired and overstimulated. The room was not wholly dark, moonlight filtered through the slatted blinds and as her eyes grew accustomed to the gloom, she could discern the various objects in the room. She turned on her side towards Clive and looked across at him. He was sleeping quietly, oblivious of her proximity. So near and yet so far, and after tomorrow she might not see him again. The next day was full of fateful possibilities; the police, or the air company, would reveal who had been on that unlucky plane and to their list would be her own name and that of whoever had been with her. Would she recognise it, she wondered, would the veil lift and reveal her past? Subconsciously she had known that tragedy lay behind it. That was why she had striven *not* to remember, but she could not hide behind it any longer. She would have to face up to whatever had happened. It would be the end of her association with Clive. The British Consul would arrange to send her home ... home? Did she possess one? The only place that was really home was the wooden house in Nuristan. There she had felt safe—so long as Clive was with her.

Her doubts and fears began to assume nightmare proportions. She sat up in bed and stared at the sleeping Clive. She wanted to wake him, she desperately needed his voice and touch to drive her bogeys away. He had never failed her yet. But he was so tired, it was not fair to burden him with her apprehensions; she had depended upon him too long. She was unsure of her exact feelings for him, she only knew that he would leave a void that it would be impossible to fill. For months their lives had mingled and he had comprised her whole horizon. With no past and a nebulous future she had clung to him as the one stable factor in her existence. She felt incapable of standing alone. The very thought caused her palms to sweat. He was still there within a few feet of her. She felt a desperate urge to creep into his arms, to feel his reassuring clasp about her. She did not recognise that it was prompted by a deeper more primitive emotion, a woman's yearning for her mate.

She slipped out of bed and crossed the space between them, and then she hesitated, recalling the glint in his eyes when he had seen her unbound hair. He might consider her action was an invitation. A reckless excitement swept over her. It did not matter if he did. If they became lovers he would never abandon her. It was a means whereby she could bind him to her. Her excuse was her desperate need of him, he did not understand how utterly lost she would be without him, and had not he connived at such a climax, when he had signed her in as Mrs Stratton?

She knelt down beside him, bringing her face level with his. Gently she touched his head, stroking the fine golden hair.

Sensing her presence, he stirred and her heart began to race with eager anticipation.

'Clive,' she whispered.

Sleepily he murmured: 'Jasmine?'

Angela recoiled as if she had been bitten by a snake. Swiftly she regained her own bed, and pulled the sheet over her head. Jasmine ... the woman in his past, the woman who she surmised had rejected him, but for whom he still hankered. Perhaps in spite of all the bitter things he had said about her sex, the breach was not beyond healing. Even now he was dreaming of her and a possible reunion. What a rebuff she had been inviting by her mad impetuosity. For one thing emerged with painful clarity—Angela the waif would never be more to him than a tiresome burden that he was anxious to relinquish, and she had been crazy to imagine otherwise.

CHAPTER FOUR

It was late when Angela awoke, having fallen into a deep sleep of exhaustion in the early hours of the morning. A waiter was placing a pot of tea beside her bed, another of the white-coated brigade that seemed to throng the hotel. He withdrew discreetly, perceiving that Angela was awake, and she sat up to drink the refreshing brew. The other bed was empty and had been made, indicating that Clive had gone out early.

The events of the previous night seemed like a hazy dream; she could not believe that she had so far forgotten herself, but the woman's name reiterated in her brain. Jasmine. Had she dreamed that too? She glanced round the room, that was concrete, so was the fact that she was in Kabul. Consulates and air agents were available to be interviewed. Today she would learn her real name, which certainly could not be Angela Stratton.

She got up and on her way to the bathroom, noticed a large cardboard box on the chaise-longue, that had not been there the night before. On top of it was a card in Clive's familiar scrawl, familiar because she had typed so many of his notes.

'I hope this meets with your approval and that it fits.'

She opened the box and found a dress and matching coat of fine wool in a shade of rich tan; there were also tights, and filmy nylon underwear; finally a pair of soft kid brown shoes. He must have gone out and bought the outfit while she still slept. Dear Clive, she thought fondly, there was no end to his kindness. Thoughtfully she picked up the underwear and regarded it. This was the sort of thing she had worn in former days ... where?

She took a shower and dressed herself in the new clothes, revelling in the feel of them. Her hair she wound about her head, pleased to see that the style made her look sophisticated. She was pale from the winter indoors and Clive's bounty did not include make-up, so she rubbed her cheeks and bit her lips in an endeavour to give them colour.

Hearing a knock upon the door, she went to open it, walking carefully, for her footgear felt strange after wearing sloppy boots so long.

Opening the door, she stared timidly at the strange man standing on the threshold. He wore a dark suit, which bore the stamp of a London tailor apparent in its excellent fit. Blue shirt and tie were immaculate, so also the fair hair slicked down to control its tendency to wave, the smoothly shaven cheeks and chin. A little overawed by so much elegance, Angela drew back, saying:

'I'm afraid I don't know ...'

A pair of mocking grey eyes smiled down into hers, eyes she could not mistake.

'Clive!' she exclaimed.

'May I come in?' he asked politely.

'Of course, it's your room too ...' She became covered in confusion. She did not know this man at all. Instead of the Viking to whom she was accustomed, she was confronted by a well-groomed man about town. Without his beard he looked much younger, and her startled eyes took in the firm lines of jaw and chin, the contours of his well-cut mouth. No longer clad in his bulky barbarian clothes, he looked slim and supple, broad of shoulder and narrow of hip.

'Well,' she gasped, 'what a metamorphosis! I didn't know you.'

'This is my normal appearance, but you look a bit flabbergasted. Doesn't it meet with your approval?'

'It's great. I ... I'd no idea you were so handsome, Clive,' she declared ingenuously.

He laughed. 'I might say the same of you.' His keen appraising glance took in her changed appearance, and a silvery glint came into his eyes. 'You're quite beautiful, Mrs Stratton.'

She caught her breath, wishing with all her heart that that name truly belonged to her. Then he would not leave her and all her problems would be solved. In addition to that, this new Clive was exciting, and the way he was looking at her caused her nerve ends to tingle.

'You know I'm not that,' she said sadly. 'Nor ever will be.'

'Don't be too sure of that.' He grinned mischievously. 'Perhaps I ought to make an honest woman of you since we've slept together.'

Recalling her mad impulse of the night before, she blushed fierily, and Clive's grin became satirical.

'Missed an opportunity, didn't we?'

Certainly this was a new Clive, and she did not know how to take him. Then she remembered Jasmine.

'Those sort of opportunities don't appeal to me,' she said coldly.

He was regarding her speculatively. 'Not really frigid, are you?'

'I'm an iceberg.' She fidgeted uncomfortably under that quizzical gaze which was making her feel nervous. She was suddenly nostalgic for her bearded friend, she had felt safe with him. A new element seemed to have entered into their relationship with the loss of Clive's hair, which made him a stranger to her.

'Shouldn't we set about discovering who I really am?' she asked.

'That might be as well,' he agreed.

But there they found themselves in an unexpected impasse. Afghan politics were very much concerned with their big and hungry neighbours along their northern borders, ever eager to infiltrate. The plane, a Russian one, had been driven off course by a sudden blizzard and had passed over forbidden territory, a military airfield, that had admitted to firing at it. It had vanished into the recesses of the Hindu Kush in a damaged condition. The incident with its international repercussions had been diplomatically smoothed over, and the authorities were anxious to forget it. The machine had been written off as lost during a storm with no survivors, and nobody wanted to reopen the enquiry. Angela's appearance was therefore embarrassing, and they disbelieved her story. If she had been on that aeroplane, they pointed out, she would know whom she had been with. A lost memory? Rubbish—temporary amnesia was understandable but not a prolonged blackout. She had an uneasy suspicion that they thought she was a spy.

The British Consul was also unhelpful. He knew Clive Stratton by name—he had a world-wide reputation as an explorer and an anthropologist—and he showed plainly that he thought his espousal of the cause of this mysterious young woman was a mistaken act of chivalry. It was very unfortunate that she had lost her memory, and about that he looked sceptical. He promised that he would endeavour to trace the passenger list of the ill-fated aircraft, but in view of the Afghans' official attitude, feared it would be un-attainable at this late date. It was very remarkable that Angela had been the only survivor, and at that point the glance he gave her was full of suspicion. Then Clive asked if he might speak to him alone, and Angela was left to her anxious conjectures. That she might be regarded as a sort of Mata Hari was a totally unexpected development and without a passport or a name, it seemed she might be faced with imprisonment, an unpleasant prospect.

Clive came back looking a little grim, but he smiled at her reassuringly, and the Consul parted from them almost cordially.

'Don't worry,' Clive told her as they stepped into the street. 'We'll find a way out.' And he relapsed into a forbidding silence, which she hesitated to break.

It was afternoon when they had concluded these frustrating interviews, and he proposed a belated lunch. She acquiesced, though in her anxiety she felt no desire for food, but he must be hungry. He maintained his silence throughout the meal and she was sure he was wondering what to do with her, and she could think of no solution herself. If he noticed her lack of appetite he made no comment, much to her relief, she did not wish to be urged to eat.

The meal concluded they walked back to the hotel, and now he did talk, pointing out various buildings and looking at her interrogatively, as if he expected her to recognise them, but she did not. Arrived at the hotel he collected the key from the desk and they went up to their room. On the threshold he hesitated and said:

'May I come in with you, I've something to say to you.'

'Of course.' She was surprised, and noticing it, he

told her:

'Last night I was too dead beat to go further afield, but I must find other accommodation now.'

Her heart sank. So he was going to abandon her, but she could not blame him. He had brought her safely back to civilisation and it was not his fault her story was disbelieved. She could expect no more from him, and possibly he had been able to persuade the Consul to send her back to England. That was what he was going to tell her.

Inside, with the door firmly closed, he looked at her keenly.

'Are you sure that you still can't remember anything? It's likely that you've been in Kabul before. Did nothing ring a bell?'

She shook her head in distress.

'Nothing. I only know that I've been in a hotel before, but that might be anywhere. And that's the truth, Clive, I wouldn't dream of deceiving you.' She put her hands over her face and trembled. 'Oh, what am I going to do?' she whispered in despair. 'What can I do? I haven't a name ... I'm just not here.'

Clive came to her and put his arms about her.

'Don't fret,' he said gently. 'You've got a name, the one I've given you, and that's the way out for you. We'll make it yours officially.'

'Clive!' She stared up into the unfamiliar face so near her own, and inconsequently thought of the Greek coin he had once shown her. There was the same straight nose and rounded chin, the slightly sensual mouth. 'What do you mean?' she went on. 'What are you saying?'

'I'm asking you to marry me, Angela.'

With a flash of pride, she demanded:

'Out of pity?'

'Not at all.' He smiled whimsically. 'We get on very well together, you type my work very efficiently, and for so long you've been called my woman, I feel you really do belong to me. I'd miss you if you weren't around.'

Not exactly the words of an ardent lover, but Angela was not critical for an enormous flood of relief had submerged her. Their abortive enquiries, the sinister hints dropped, had filled her with dismay. She knew she was in a predicament from which she could not possibly extricate herself by her own efforts. That he did not intend to desert her delighted her.

'You don't know,' she began, her voice breaking, 'how much your offer means to me. But ... but can we be married, not knowing who I am?'

'I think a point or two can be stretched, since everyone is so anxious to be rid of you.' He stroked her hair gently.

'I ... I was afraid they'd lock me up.'

'The authorities would much rather hand you over to me, if I'll take you out of the country unobtrusively. There's a British Mission in Kabul, we'll find a priest there.'

'But ... we don't know ... suppose I've been married before?'

'We'll chance that. Somehow I'm quite sure you've not.'

Angela stood within the circle of his arms, her head against his shoulder, and felt safe. She more than suspected his offer had been made out of a chivalrous desire to protect her, she could not imagine that he was in love with her, but since she had come to rely upon him utterly, she could not face the wrench of parting from him. She was ready to snatch at any loophole he offered to remain with him and that he had miraculously offered to marry her was almost too good to be true, so she would not quibble about his motives. Soothed and comforted, she murmured:

'You're so good, so generous. There's nothing in the world I wouldn't do for you and it'll be just heaven to be your wife.'

He laughed derisively. 'What a child you are, Angela! I'm not offering you eternal bliss. You may find me far from easy to live with. I'm thirty-six, you know, and a bit set in my ways.'

With adoration in her eyes, she said: 'Your ways shall be my ways.'

'That'll suit me fine,' he said ironically. 'I'll take you up on that.'

With his arm still around her, he guided her to the chaise-longue and seated himself beside her. Releasing her, he sought for his cigarettes and matches.

'I mean it, Clive,' she insisted. 'If ... later on ... you want to go off to Timbuctoo or some place off the map, I ... I wouldn't mind, and I'd hate you to feel tied.'

He smiled cynically; he had heard women make similar statements when they were out to capture his more adventurous friends, but once married they had found it impossible to get away.

'That's very sweet of you,' he told her, 'but my wandering days are over. I've had a good innings, but I intend to go home and settle down.' He stubbed out his cigarette and turned to look at her. 'As soon as we can get a visa for you we'll return to England. But don't you want to ask any questions? You don't even know if I'm in a position to support a wife.'

'I ... I hadn't thought about it, and I trust you implicitly.'

'How nice!' He searched her face and seemed satisfied with what he saw. 'Actually I'm not badly off, the place in Dorset provides a comfortable income.'

Angela's brow wrinkled in distress as a new thought presented itself. 'But you're having to take me on trust. For all we know my relations might be criminals.'

He laughed wholeheartedly. 'You don't look a criminal type, my dear, but when we get to London I want you to consult a psychiatrist.'

'Whatever for?'

'Because I'm sure your trouble is psychological, not physical. Unconsciously you're deliberately retarding your recovery. You don't *want* to remember anything that happened before the accident, and so your subconscious suppresses your efforts to recall your past.'

Angela flushed angrily. 'That can't be so, Clive. I'm not neurotic. Of course I want to know who I am.'

'You think you do, but you don't really. You've had a traumatic experience, perhaps more than one and you shrink from the pain of remembrance. But I hope by the time it is recalled to you, you'll be feeling so secure with me that the wounds will have healed.'

Angela nervously pleated her skirt. He was only too right—she had shrunk from delving into her past.

'I want my life to begin with meeting you,' she said obstinately.

'It didn't, you know, but you can't have had a lot before then, you're so young. I, I'm afraid, have had a good deal.'

A shadow crossed his face and Angela recalled the name he had spoken in his sleep.

'Clive, who is Jasmine?' she asked abruptly.

He stared at her bleakly, his eyes becoming like ice. 'Who mentioned her?'

'You did. Last night, while you were asleep.'

His face broke into a rueful smile. 'I'm sorry I was so

indiscreet.'

'But who is she?' Angela persisted, chill creeping over her joy. At his age he must have had former attachments, but did this Jasmine have a claim upon him?

He lit another cigarette, and proceeded to blow smoke rings, watching them ascend with concentration, his face a mask. Angela waited with increasing apprehension. Obviously he was unwilling to speak of the other girl. At length he sighed and told her:

'You'd better know. Someone else will tell you if I don't. Jasmine was my wife.'

'You've been married before?'

'Briefly.' He looked round for the ashtray. 'She died nine years ago,' he said bluntly.

Angela drew a long breath. So she had no living rival to fear—but he must have loved Jasmine very deeply if she still came to him in his dreams.

'It was after that I started roaming,' he went on. 'I had to get away for a while, and then it became a habit.'

Angela digested this information. So the real reason for his wandering foot was to find assuagement for the loss of a much loved wife. Strange, though, that he had spoken so bitterly of women if he had cared so much.

Clive glanced at her thoughtful face and took a long drag at his cigarette.

'I'm afraid I'm past the romantic age,' he said apologetically. 'All my illusions died with Jasmine, but at least I'll be able to take good care of you, and I think that's what you need.'

'You always have,' she told him gratefully, though she felt a little dashed; she wanted a husband, not a father.

He continued to smoke in silence and she watched

68

him furtively, noticing how attractively his eyelashes curled at the ends. She wanted to touch them with her fingertips, but she was a little shy of this changed Clive, and she was sure he would find such a caress juvenile. She said naïvely:

'Did you love ... your wife ... very much?'

He smiled wryly. 'I don't think the feelings Jasmine aroused could be called love, which emotion I understand should be selfless. Of course I was a silly young fool who thought all women were angels. Jasmine was hardly that, she ...' a faraway look came into his eyes ... 'was a flame of a woman, very beautiful and exciting ...' His voice faded out and he relapsed into brooding silence, while Angela wished she had held her tongue. It gave her no comfort to learn that Jasmine had been a flaming beauty and exciting, which she herself was certainly not.

'So for nine years you're exiled yourself for her sake,' she said sorrowfully.

'Like you I had memories I wanted to forget,' he pointed out. 'But I've been home from time to time.' He turned towards her with a kindling warmth in his grey eyes. 'But that's all over and done with. Together you and I will exorcise our ghosts.'

'I'm sure I hope we can,' she said a little doubtfully. Jasmine sounded as if she would take a lot of laying. 'But hadn't you better tell me what your family consists of? You said you had a mother, is there anyone else?'

'Only Ralph, my half-brother. He works with computers, but the Sherborne firm he's with doesn't give him enough scope. He wants to go to London. I found a letter from him waiting for me here. He says Mother is in difficulties, though she won't admit it; the business of the estate is becoming too complicated for her to cope with, and he's tired of acting as my deputy. So I must go back and put things to rights and assume my responsibilities.' He paused, then went on: 'Perhaps I should elucidate a little further. Mother isn't my real mother—she died at my birth. My father married again, a widow with an infant daughter. Both needed a home, so it seemed to be a good arrangement. Celia has always treated me like her own son, and I've always called her Mother. Ralph came along much later, and being the baby of the family got thoroughly spoiled.' He smiled fondly; evidently he was very attached to his half-brother.

'Then who's there now?' Angela asked, a little daunted by such a complicated family history, and the prospect of meeting strangers who might not welcome a young girl whom Clive had married so quixotically, and had nothing to recommend her, not even a name.

'Oh, just Mother and Ralph. My father died some years back. He was a good deal older than Celia.'

That did not sound too frightening. Only an elderly woman and a young man with whom to cope. Yet she was aware of a sudden inexplicable dread of going to the Stratton home and sharing Clive with his relations. He had lived there with this Jasmine, who seemed to have been a fascinating creature, and the place was so impregnated with memories of her that he had been unable to stay there for long since her death. He talked confidently about laying her ghost, but she must be a very potent spirit because he still dreamed of her.

'Is it essential that we go back to England?' Angela asked. 'I ... I don't remember what the country's like, I think I've always lived in a town. Even Afghanistan would be more like home.'

'I'm afraid we must, and I don't think we'd be allowed to stay here. Your appearance seems to have caused a flutter in high places. But we shan't be going tomorrow, nor the day after. We have to get married first and have our papers put in order. Meanwhile you'll need some more clothes.' He pulled a roll of notes out of his pocket and threw them into her lap. 'There's an English lady, a Mrs Newcome, staying in the hotel who I'm sure will be pleased to show you the best shops.' Seeing protest in her face, he went on quickly, 'Feminine purchases are not my cup of tea. I felt a fool going into that store this morning, especially when it came to buying the undies, but the salesgirl was very helpful. The things I do for you!'

'I appreciate it.' She flushed as she picked up the notes. 'But I don't like taking all this, Clive.'

'Why ever not? You must be properly dressed. Damn it all, you're my wife, or very nearly.'

He sprang up and walking to the window stood looking out. 'You'll require nightwear, including slippers. You went barefoot last night, but that I felt was beyond me.'

Angela's colour deepened. In her intense relief, she had overlooked the more intimate aspect of their new relationship. Clive had presented himself as her guardian and protector and she half suspected that that was all he meant to be. She eyed his broad back doubtfully. She had asked if he had offered out of pity, and he had returned lightly that he had become used to having her around, and she was an efficient typist. Except for those few moments by his bedside of which he knew nothing and she was now very much ashamed, their connection had been almost sexless. He had not so much as kissed her.

She said hesitantly: 'You've been awfully kind and generous, Clive, and I'm deeply grateful, but there's no need to burden yourself with me permanently. I rather think you're marrying me to get me out of the country, as there seems no other way, but once I'm safe in England, we can easily part if the marriage isn't ... I mean ... if we don't ...'

'You mean a marriage in name only?' he asked in an odd voice.

'Well, yes: it isn't as if ...' She had been going to say we were in love, but the words died on her lips as he swung round to face her, his appearance completely changed. His brows were contracted over eyes which held a smouldering fire, an almost avid look, and there was something menacing about the set of his mouth.

'Am I physically repulsive to you?' he demanded.

'Oh, no, Clive, I didn't mean that,' she cried in distress.

'Perhaps before we go any further, we'd better make sure,' he said ominously. 'I'm not going to be cheated again.'

Cheated? What could he mean? Was he referring to the previous night? But he did not know that she had knelt beside him in palpitating expectancy until he had uttered Jasmine's name. He gave her no chance to ask him, striding across the room towards her and pulling her to her feet and up against him. His mouth came down on hers as his arms enclosed her in a hungry embrace, that made it difficult to breathe, much less escape. Not that she had any wish to do so, for as his kisses became more demanding, she took fire from him. Her slight body moulded itself into the lean muscular strength of his, her lips parted under the pressure of his lips. His impatient fingers loosened the zip at the back of her dress, and as neck and shoulders became exposed, his mouth wandered over them, returning to hers. Her hair fell about them, its soft waves enveloping them. Finally he lifted her and laid her on her bed, his hands moving over her quivering body. Then with an effort he mastered his passion, straightening himself and moving away.

'No ... not yet,' he muttered thickly, breathing fast, and returned to the window.

Angela lay still while the tumult in her blood subsided and her racing pulses slowly returned to their normal rate. She had been taken completely by surprise, and not only Clive's violence but her own passionate response had astounded her. Of one thing she was certain, never in her shrouded past had she had such an experience. Dimly she was aware that there had been somebody who had kissed her, but the memory was painful and she wanted to forget it ... had forgotten it until now.

This new facet of Clive's character was a little shattering. She had never thought of him before as a passionate man, and his embrace had been ruthlessly demanding, without any tenderness, which surely should be a part of love. Did he love her? Did she love him? She did not know, but he was tinder to her fire.

Sitting up, she pushed back her heavy hair and asked a little shakily:

'Are you satisfied now?'

He turned round and regarded her quizzically, with a flicker of flame still in his eyes.

'Not in the least, but I can wait. Well, we've ascertained that you're not the iceberg you declared yourself. I think our marriage will work.'

The coldbloodedness of that assertion offended her. She slid off the bed and went to the mirror to arrange her hair.

'You mean from the physical standpoint?' she asked coldly.

73

'Which happens to be rather important.' He strolled towards her, his hands in his pockets. The flame had left his eyes and he showed no sign of his previous emotion. She burst out angrily:

'Marriage isn't a problem in physics.'

'Biologically mutual attraction is a question of chemistry,' he returned imperturbably. In the mirror she saw him smile wryly: 'I've all the natural man's susceptibility to a beautiful woman.'

'But I'm not beautiful.'

'I find you so.'

That ought to have caused her elation, but it did not. How quickly he switched off, and how calculating his lovemaking had been, a test of her reactions. He had wanted to make sure that she was not frigid and after a winter of monkish abstinence he was eager for a responsive woman. She had an uncomfortable suspicion that any woman could have satisfied him, and that was not love.

'I don't like the way you talk,' she protested. 'You make me feel as if I were qualifying for a harem!'

She remembered that he had said all women should be confined in zenanas, and suspected that they were of such small importance in his man's world that they were only necessary to fill a basic need.

Clive noticed the despondent droop of her shoulders and said gently:

'I'm sorry, Angela, I'm forgetting how young you are. You think I'm crude and insensitive ... Oh, yes, you do.' At her quick movement of dissent. 'You want all the romantic trimmings, declarations of undying devotion.' He sighed. 'I'm afraid I can't rise to flowery phrases. I'm too old and disillusioned. I feel that from me they'd sound ridiculous, and for the most part they're insincere.'

She said a little tartly, for she was not a naïve teenager, who swallowed pretty speeches as a proof of love:

'Your trouble is you've lived too long out East. You think like an oriental. A wife should share her husband's life and not only his bed.'

'I quite agree,' he told her unexpectedly. 'I'm hoping you'll give me ... co-operation.'

Co-operation? What a word to use when what she wanted was to hear an avowal of love, but that emotion seemed beyond his range. What did he mean by it? An acceptance of his explorations? She had already promised she would not seek to keep him from those. Or a united front to fight a phantom? Jasmine, of course. He had given his first wife all the love of which he was capable and he could not love again. All he could offer to her were the embers of a fire long burned out, that was what he meant when he said he was too old and disillusioned for romance. Well, the embers had been hot enough, and with patience and understanding she might be able to fan them into a purer flame than mere desire.

'I'll do my best to make you a good wife,' she said primly, hoping that she sounded adult; though there was so much more she wanted to say, she did not wish to appear like a soppy schoolgirl.

He smiled, the mocking smile that she was beginning to hate.

'Don't try too hard or you'll make me feel self-conscious,' he advised lightly. 'Be your natural self, my dear, and we'll make out. Oh, we'll have our ups and downs like most couples, but we'll weather them, I don't doubt, with mutual tolerance.'

An observation that she found extremely irritating.

He began to move about the room, collecting his things.

'I'll just take my bits and pieces,' he went on, putting them in a bag. 'I'm staying at the English Club until we're married. As for the stuff we brought from Nuristan, I'll make a donation of it to the waiters. They'll have relations who would be glad of it.'

Alarmed, she asked anxiously: 'You're leaving me alone here?'

'I'll drop in for meals. I can't book another room in this hotel—they'd think it odd, since you're supposed to be Mrs Stratton.'

She panicked, terrified that he might after all be going to desert her.

'Why can't you go on sharing this room? We did last night.'

Clive shot her an oblique glance. 'After what's just happened it would be too great a strain upon our virtue,' he remarked drily.

'But does it matter?'

'My dear girl, I'm surprised at you.' He pretended to be shocked. Then he said more seriously. 'I think it does, Angela, in case there's a hitch.'

'Meaning we mightn't be able to get married after all?'

'Oh, I'm sure we shall,' he said quickly, a little too quickly. 'But we ought to wait until the padre's had his say, don't you agree?'

She concurred without enthusiasm, dreading separation even though it would be only temporary, as she assured herself feverishly.

He picked up the bag.

'See you later in the lounge,' he said casually. 'And we'll arrange that shopping expedition with Mrs Newcome. We'll tell her you lost your luggage *en route*.' He moved towards the door, and she watched him dumbly; she was in such a state of nerves, she could

76

hardly bear him out of her sight.

On the threshold, he turned back to her with again that mocking smile.

'Get yourself something glamorous to delight my eyes upon our wedding night.'

'Oh, you! You sultan!' she exploded.

He laughed and went out, without offering to kiss her goodbye.

Angela stared at the closed door a little resentfully. He could not be more casual if they had been married for years. Perhaps that was it, they had been together too long and too intimately for courtship. But she felt defrauded. Most of what he had said to her was, she supposed, good sense, and he had been honest, but it was meagre diet for a hungry heart.

CHAPTER FIVE

MRS NEWCOME was a lively widow who was doing a tour of the Middle East. An early riser, she had seen Clive go out in the morning, bearded and bulky, and return transformed, carrying Angela's box of clothes. She pumped the reception clerk, and having ascertained his name and occupation, waited for him to come down to breakfast, which, having found Angela still sleeping, he did. Seating herself at the next table to his, she introduced herself, pretending a great admiration for his books, of which she had never heard previously and had certainly never read.

Clive was at first unresponsive, until it occurred to

him that she might be of help to Angela, and he then
unbent. When Angela came down to dinner that evening, he presented her to the widow, and the shopping
expedition was arranged for the following morning.

Mrs Newcome was small, plump, and vicacious, with
buxom good looks. She was in her early forties with
brown hair and inquisitive hazel eyes, alert to probe
her neighbour's business.

'Since I lost my poor Albert, I don't seem able to
settle down,' she confided to Angela. 'Fortunately he
left me enough to indulge my restlessness. You see, we
had no family, which I don't regret—modern youth is
too much for a lone widow woman to cope with.'

Next day she conducted Angela into the new town
with its modern shops, and wide avenues. The dark
alleys of the bazaars behind the waterfront, though
more intriguing, were not safe, she insisted, for two
unprotected women.

Kabul is not a distinguished town; it sprawls along
its straggling river without shape or architectural style.
In spring the river is a raging torrent, but in summer
it shrinks to a series of stagnant pools in which its
population simultaneously pray, wash clothes, water
camels, and relieve themselves. At the time of Angela's
visit the river had begun to recede and its residents
foregather on its banks. One thing is beautiful; though
Kabul is situated on a plain, there is a vista of mountains at the end of every street, the vanguard of the
several ranges that ring the city.

Knowing that the summer would be before her
when she reached England, Angela bought thin trousers and tops, several light dresses and the necessary
underwear and nightdresses. Clive, she was sure, would
not appreciate pyjamas. Remembering his parting injunction with a blush, she was extravagant over a dia-

phanous negligée. Mrs Newcome was lavish with advice and suggestions, but her taste was all for frills and fussiness, whereas Angela liked plain styles. Of all she bought, it was only the negligée of which her companion really approved.

Over coffee and cakes in a very westernised café their conversation inevitably turned towards Clive, with whom the widow was obviously smitten.

'You are lucky, my dear, to have such a charming man,' she said enviously. 'And so good-looking.'. Privately she thought he had thrown himself away upon Angela. The girl was handsome, but so young and gauche. She had looked sceptically at Angela's ringless hands, for that was a detail Clive had overlooked, and Angela had told her a little lamely that she had lost her wedding ring.

'As well as your luggage? Dear me, you were unfortunate,' Mrs Newcome had exclaimed, obviously disbelieving that she had ever had one. However, the widow prided herself upon being a woman of the world, and not easily shocked, and she was wondering if Clive could be detached from his liaison with this girl whose naïveté must surely be beginning to pall. So she set herself to find out all she could about this incongruous couple, and was a little disappointed when Angela told her they would be leaving for England within a few days' time.

'Just when I was getting to know you. It's so seldom that one meets really compatible people,' Mrs Newcome said with emphasis. 'We'll have to make the most of what time we have together.'

Angela thought Clive had made a mistake by encouraging this woman whom she did not find compatible at all, but he had so much to do he was glad to know that Angela had company. Her exit visa entailed several interviews with various officials and there was the wedding arrangements to make, beside some private business, so he had to leave her very much alone.

At lunch Mrs Newcome managed to get herself transferred to their table in the hotel dining room and did what she could to monopolise Clive's attention. The waiters winked at each other covertly. The Sahib was getting himself another wife, he must be rich enough to support two, and this second one, though a little mature, was much more bedworthy by their standards. She would keep the little one in order, and it was all humbug that the British were monogamists.

Angela watched Mrs Newcome's eye-play and wondered if Clive were impressed. She was not exactly jealous, but she did not enjoy the widow's blatant advances; Clive, she thought, responded a little too readily to her sallies. She wondered if his susceptibility to women extended to others beside herself.

At dinner time, catching sight of the widow firmly esconced at their table, she waited in the foyer to waylay Clive as he came in.

'I don't know why you had to ask her to join us,' she complained. 'I want you to myself.'

'I don't think I did,' he returned, 'she asked herself.' He gave her a narrow glance. 'Don't start becoming possessive, Angela. I won't stand for it, and I should have thought you'd had enough of my sole company.'

Nettled by his tone, she began sharply: 'Of course if you're tired of me already . . .'

He interrupted her. 'That's enough, Angela. Mrs Newcome has been very kind looking after you while I have to be out.'

'I'm not a baby, or do you think I need a duenna?' she asked heatedly. 'I think she suspects we aren't married.'

'That's soon going to be remedied.' His hand closed on her arm in a vicelike grip. 'Come in to dinner and behave yourself. This evening I'm going to take you to visit some Pushtu friends of mine. They may be an object lesson to you.'

Angela was so ruffled she was about to tell him she did not want an object lesson and he could go and visit his friends by himself, but realising that she would be left to her own devices, she checked herself in time. At least Mrs Newcome would be left behind.

Ayoub Khan lived in an old house on a mountainside above the city. Angela and Clive were ushered into a dim, cool room, lit by kerosene lamps in beautiful wrought iron brackets, dispersing a mellow glow over the rich rugs and piled cushions on the floor. At one end was a raised divan with more cushions. Their host came to greet them, a man of about fifty wearing a Western suit and a karacul hat. He embraced Clive affectionately—apparently they were old friends—and bowed ceremoniously to Angela. Various other men appeared, sons, nephews ... Angela never discovered who was who. She had an impression of flashing dark eyes in aquiline faces. They all conversed in Pushtu, which Angela could not understand. Only when they had all been presented did the women of the household appear, as was customary bringing a white cloth to lay upon the floor, the inevitable tea, and sweetmeats, and large bowls of pistachio nuts.

One of the young men introduced Angela to a handsome middle-aged woman, wearing a sort of white sari about her head and shoulders—'My mother,' he said in English—then a much younger woman, also with her head covered, though none of them were veiled. 'My other mother.' The two ladies sat on either side of their husband on the divan, the others grouped them-

selves about the room. Angela found she was expected
to sit cross-legged upon cushions on the floor, and she
hoped her tights would not run and she was not showing too much leg. Then the young children were
brought in to be shown to the visitors, toddlers and
even babies. All were quiet and well behaved as Moslem children are taught to be. Angela had no idea as
to who belonged to whom, or how many families the
patriarchal roof sheltered. Ayoub Khan was definitely
a patriarch, smiling benignly upon all and sundry, but
there seemed to be no friction. An atmosphere of calm
happiness and security pervaded the whole family, and
both wives had an air of smiling serenity.

A girl came to sit beside Angela, anxious to show off
her English. She had learned it, she said, at school,
which she had permission to attend. Education was being extended to girls, though it was not yet universal.
'I hope,' she said, 'to become a teacher, though
eventually I expect to marry.'

Her eyes went to Clive, who had retreated into a
corner with one of the elder men and was discussing
Afghan politics, with occasional interpolations from
their host.

'So that is your man,' she said. 'You are fortunate to
have such a fine one. He might even make a Buzkashi
player.'

Angela had to confess ignorance of Buzkashi, and
her companion hastened to enlighten her. It was the
national game of Afghanistan, a sort of polo played
with a headless goat instead of a ball. The horsemen
struggled for possession of the carcase, which once ob-
tained had to be hauled across their saddles, and carried so many times round the field before being de-
posited in a pit. But the horseman was intercepted by
other players, and fierce battles took place, in which

the horses joined. Afghans were superb horsemen, the finest in the world.

'We girls make the players our heroes,' the girl said, her great dark eyes flashing. 'No languishing Indian film stars for us. I have pictures of all the famous ones.'

'Pin-ups?' Angela suggested.

The girl giggled. 'That is so, all round the room I share with my sisters. Pin-ups.' She repeated the word, seeming pleased with this addition to her vocabulary. 'A man should be arrogantly male,' she asserted.

'Oh, quite,' Angela agreed, a little out of her depth. She glanced at Clive. Did her companion see him as arrogantly male? He was autocratic at times, but she did not think he had much in common with these savage horsemen whom the Afghan girl so much admired.

As it was a fine night, Clive suggested that they should walk back to the city, and eager to prolong her time in his company, Angela concurred. They walked along arm in arm discussing the harmony that seemed to exist in Ayoub Khan's motley household.

'But I should hate to have to share you with another woman,' Angela remarked.

'Most women do share their husbands,' Clive returned cynically, 'though they don't know it. In Moslem countries there are no spinsters, which is all to the good.'

'On the principle that half a man is better than none?' Angela suggested.

'Definitely, and they have their children to fulfil themselves.'

'Do you then sponsor polygamy?'

'Not at all, and in any case it's dying out for economic reasons—men can't support more than one wife. But Eastern women, unlike their Western sisters, still regard the family as the be-all and end-all of their lives.'

'Perhaps they won't when they're better educated.'

'A pity if education is going to make them discontented.'

'Yours is a very masculine point of view, isn't it, Clive?'

'After all, I'm a man,' he observed drily, 'and you must admit the Ayoub family seemed very happy.'

'Yes, well, they're Afghans,' Angela said vaguely. She was recalling that Clive had had another wife and he still regretted her. As if he sensed her thought, he said:

'A man can care for two women, Angela, without lessening his feeling for either.'

Moonlight was painting the mountains that ringed the city in black and silver, a vast horizon wild and free like the spirit of its people. Angela pressed the arm she held affectionately. He was trying to tell her that although Jasmine had had the love of his youth, he had room in his heart for her too. Jasmine had been dead nine years and all the future was hers.

They were married at the British Mission. Angela gave her maiden name as Nunn, which but for the spelling was correct—parents unknown. Regarding her date of birth she told Clive she was sure that she had been born in the spring. She had some hazy recollection of a big party with the table decorated with spring flowers, tulips predominating. The wild ones in Afghanistan had rung a bell.

'And I think I must be twenty-one,' she said. 'That was why it was such a big do.'

Though twenty-one had rather lost its significance with the lowering of the coming of age to eighteen, Angela looked too mature for eighteen, so she decided it must have been her twenty-first. Her speech was definitely British, and that was all the meagre information she could supply about herself. Clive gave her birthday as March the twenty-first, the first day of spring, and hoped he was not perjuring himself. He gave Angela another ring, besides her wedding one, an Egyptian scarab, and a necklace of lapis lazuli, because that stone was mined in Afghanistan, and it was to be a memento of their stay there.

'I didn't think you were sentimental,' she said when she had thanked him.

'No more I am, but I thought it would be appropriate,' he told her hastily. He seemed to think it was a crime to betray any sentiment.

Over the scarab, she bent her brows; it seemed to have familiar associations.

'I wonder if my people were interested in archaeology,' she observed. 'Perhaps I really did come here on a dig.'

Clive looked black. 'I hope not,' his tone was curt. 'I don't like archaeologists.' But he refused to tell her why.

After the simple ceremony, he moved back into her room, at the hotel, and during a night of pain and rapture, Angela had proof that she had not been married before. Clive's lovemaking was alternately fierce and tender, and when day dawned, Angela disengaged herself from his arms on the narrow bed that they had shared, with the full knowledge that she loved him deeply and irrevocably. She left him to sleep while she took her shower, and her heart sang a paean of triumphant joy. She was his and he was hers, and nothing should ever part them.

Breakfast had been ordered to be sent up to their room; neither were in the mood to encounter Mrs

Newcome. When it had been eaten, and Clive had gone to shave, Angela idly leafed through some pictures of the high spots in Afghanistan issued by the Afghan Tourist Board feeling pleasantly languid. She came upon a large picture of the colossal Buddha at Bamian. It was carved in a niche in the mountain wall, which was honeycombed with ancient cells once inhabited by religious monks, for Bamian had been a great centre of Buddhism, thronged with priests and pilgrims, until Genghis Khan and his hordes came over the Oxus and devastated the country in 1221. Bamian had been particularly unfortunate. Situated in a long valley, it was guarded by two fortified cities at each end. These had refused to surrender to the Mongols and in the battle for their possession, the great Khan's favourite grandson had been shot by an arrow. In revenge, the grieving grandfather had proclaimed that no living thing was to be left alive in the valley, and so it was. Every man, woman and child, beast and bird were slaughtered, even the trees were cut down, the barley slashed from its root. The valley became a place of desolation, it was considered accursed, and for a hundred years it was totally abandoned. When eventually men crept back to take up life there, they built little farming villages among neat fields. But the two great figures of the Buddha, one much smaller than the other, were still there, though defaced and mutilated, now objects of interest to the archaeologists who were beginning to throng Afghanistan to excavate the centuries of history that were buried in its soil.

Some vague memories of Bamian's story filtered back into Angela's consciousness as she stared at the picture. She called to Clive excitedly:

'Clive, I know that place! I've been there. I recognise the statue.'

He came to join her and looked from the print to her flushed face. He had always expected that some association would eventually recall her past to her, and this might be it.

'We must go there,' he decided promptly. 'Our flight is booked for two days hence, so if we start at once we can spend a night there and be back in time to catch it.'

Angela's mood changed as apprehension submerged her first excitement.

'Don't let's bother,' she said quickly. She was so happy in her new life, she dreaded a revelation that might mar it. Some premonition warned her that the discovery of her identity might be a threat to it.

But Clive was determined to go. If Bamian could restore Angela's memory it would be better than any psychiatric probings. Reluctantly Angela allowed her misgivings to be overruled.

Clive had hired a car and as soon as they were dressed, they set off. The spring rains were past, and the sky was blue and cloudless. The road led through the Kop-i-daman valley. Along one side of it were mountains, brown and grey, criss crossed with a faint tracery of shepherds' trails beaten hard by the countless hoofs of the herds. On the other side were neatly laid out fields, each rimmed with a low mud wall and laced with little irrigation ditches. Against the treeless landscape, kingfishers flashed like bits of iridescent enamel and big black and white magpies sauntered through the fields.

They passed Istalif, with green woods tucked into a ravine, and stopped at Charikar to buy kebabs from the bazaar, lamb and young kid, crisp and smoking, and slabs of fresh bread. Then they turned west into the gorge of the Ghorband river. The road lay along the bottom of a deep slot carved by the water between sheer cliffs, the stream running beside it. Thence over the Shibar Pass and on towards Bamian. A few miles before reaching the mouth of the valley, Clive pulled up in the dusty road at the foot of a mountain and pointed to an overgrown pathway winding upward. On the cliffs above her, Angela could discern crumbling turrets and desolate walls.

'Shar-i-Golgola,' Clive told her, 'the city of Clamour and Lamentation. It was one of the two built at either end to protect the valley, and it has never been rebuilt since Genghis Khan destroyed it. It's said that in the night those broken towers echo with the wails of the doomed who were murdered there.'

Angela shivered; the red sandstone walls of the gorge behind them were flushed in the red light of the sinking sun to the colour of blood. Her face was white and strained, for throughout the journey she had been strung to recall whether she had passed that way before. Certain features appeared to be familiar, like scenes seen in a dream. Also she seemed always to have known the story of Bamian's destruction. Would the great Buddha bring everything back to her, and how was she going to react? Whoever had been with her on that unlucky plane had met with a destruction as complete as the ruined city above them.

Clive glanced at her a little anxiously, wondering if he were putting too great a strain upon her, but it was essential that Angela should discover who she really was, if they were not to be faced with continuing embarrassments and uncertainties.

The light was fading as they reached Bamian itself and drew up at the hotel, which was on top of a low hill directly opposite to the Buddhist ruins across the valley. Clive decreed that they should call it a day and they went in to partake of the dinner, which the manager, who had been advised of their coming by telephone, had set for them in a screened-off portion of the dining room. The hotel was full of campers of various nationalities who had been up to Band-i-Amil, the mysterious lakes in the heart of mountainous desert, which had no visible source or origin nor for the fish that swam in them. The Strattons dined on trout that had been brought down from them.

When they sought their beds, Angela stood for a long time at the window looking across the valley to the sculptured cliff. There was a full moon and the two great figures, tiny from that distance, were visible like rods of metal in the shadow of their niches.

Again she was convinced that she had stood in that same window before and gazed at that scene, but how, when, and with whom still eluded her.

Clive watched her from the bed, unwilling to intrude upon her vigil which might bear such fruitful results. He had blown out the lamp and only the eerie moonlight illuminated the room. Angela in her long wrap over her nightdress was like a wraith herself in the pale light, except for her black hair streaming over her shoulders.

At length he spoke.

'Come to bed, dear, you'll be getting frozen. We'll visit Colossus in the morning.'

His voice broke the spell that enwrapped her. Shivering, she turned from the window and groped her way to the bed.

'I ... I don't think we should. I wish we hadn't come.'

'That's cowardly, Angela. Now we're here we must go through with it.'

Naturally he was hoping for results. Clive would like to know whom he had married and her fears were stupid. Whatever was about to be revealed must be faced for his sake if not for her own.

Fears and apprehensions vanished in the safety of his arms.

In the morning they stood half way up the cliff at the foot of the bigger colossus, looking up beyond the gigantic legs, the drapery, the shattered arms to the blind face far overhead, originally covered with gold leaf, that had long disappeared, and the colours weathered away. Of the frescoes which had decorated the niche, there were only faded fragments left, high up in the arched dome. The statue had been mutilated, much of the face, the hands and limbs had been blasted away by zealous Moslem sharpshooters bent upon idol breaking. The mouth and chin remained intact, curved in a serene smile The whole cliff into which it was carved was pocked with empty niches and entrances to the hundreds of chambers within, for here had once lived a whole colony of monks.

Angela held Clive's hand clutched in hers while her eyes wandered over the pink cliffs and back again to the Buddha. She knew it all, she had stood here before, staring up at the image with awe and wonder, hand in hand with another man. Suddenly his face swam before her vision, a lean lined face with dark eyes like her own and a thatch of silver hair. She heard his voice say:

'It's funny, isn't it, that so much that has been built by man to the glory of God has been despoiled by other men, also in the name of a god.'

'Daddy!' she gasped. 'Oh, Daddy!'

Clive put his arm around her. 'You were here with your father?'

'Yes. We'd been on a dig in Persia—I told you I thought I had some connection with archaeology, and Daddy was an excavator of some note. He wanted to have a look at the northern cities, so we came in by Herat, and went to Balkh—that's very old, isn't it?'

'Very old,' he said soothingly, unwilling to hurry her.

'We came down there, and went back, finally reaching Qizil Qala, intending to fly down to Kabul. I hadn't been to Kabul ... then ...' Her voice died away.

Clive held her gently, stroking her head, but she did not weep, for she had always known that in that accident she had been bereft, but other memories were thronging back. She had gone on that dig not because she had been interested in archaeology, she never had been, but because she had needed distraction. He mother had died after a long illness through which she had nursed her. Arthur had promised to wait for her, for she had felt she could not desert her parent and the end was inevitable. But it was too long in coming for Arthur. He had grown impatient and married another girl, or perhaps he had never really loved her. Doubly bereft, her father had taken her with him to Persia, and now he had gone too.

'I've no one left,' she said distractedly.

'You've got me,' Clive reminded her. 'Come back to the hotel and lie down. I think a sedative would be a good idea.'

He led her away, guiding her over the stones and fallen masonry. She walked blindly, relying upon his supporting arm, her mind absorbed in her recollections. She had thought that she had loved Arthur, he had been her mainstay during those months of her mother's illness, and all the while he had been two-timing her. But even as she remembered him, he seemed infinitely remote, and she wondered how he had been able to cause her so much pain. But at the time when she had discovered his perfidy, she had walked into a desert of desolation, her future a blank, and death with her father in that ravine would have been welcome. But Clive had brought her back to life and love, a deeper and far more profound emotion, because she was more mature. She said suddenly:

'You won't ever desert me, Clive?'

Surprised, he answered: 'Of course not, my dear, whatever made you say that?'

'Because there was someone who did. Oh, I was only engaged to him, but ... but ...' her lip quivered.

'So that was the trouble? But forget it, dear. Now you can really put the past away and look forward to a new life. I'll try to make up to you for all you've lost in the old.'

'Oh, you will, I know you will.'

How infinitely kind and comforting he could be.

He said after a while: 'Were you very devoted to your father?'

'I adored him, but I didn't see very much of him. His work was always taking him away. Archaeology was his passion. Mother always declared he thought more of ruins than of living people.'

'Yes,' he returned with sudden violence. 'That sort of thing can become a mania, causing a man to neglect his nearest ties.'

Fleetingly Angela recalled that Clive too had an obsession that might take him away from her, but he had said he would never desert her.

'I don't think Mother and Dad got on awfully well,' she told him. 'They only kept together because of me, and then, when I became grown up, she was so ill. I nursed her.'

'You don't seem to have had much of a life, my poor waif,' Clive commented kindly. 'We'll hope there are better things in store for you.'

Arrived back at the hotel, he insisted that she should lie down and he would give her a sedative.

'You need to adjust to your newly discovered past,' he told her. 'A long sleep would help.'

Glass in one hand and pills in the other, he approached the bed upon which she was lying. 'Incidentally, have you remembered your name?'

'My name? Why, of course—it's Ann, and that's not unlike Angela.' She resolved that she would always use the latter name; it was the one Clive had given her and doubly precious upon that account.

'But your surname,' Clive persisted. 'That's more important.'

She knitted her brows. 'Something beginning with S.' She paused considering. 'Sullivan,' she announced triumphantly. 'That's it, I'm Ann Sullivan!'

She looked up, expecting congratulation, and saw Clive had turned very white. He hurriedly put the glass down beside her.

'Sullivan,' he echoed in a curious strangled voice. 'Oh, no! Not Edmund Sullivan?'

'That's right.' Puzzled, she stared at him. 'You ... you've heard of him?'

'Yes, he was quite an eminent man in his line.' He still spoke with difficulty. 'Didn't he head an expedition to Greece some ten years ago to look for Argive tombs? There were some rather unruly students in his team.'

'I wouldn't know, I was only a schoolgirl then, but he often did take students—he liked to encourage young people.'

'He did that all right,' Clive said with such bitter

meaning that Angela was more and more bewildered. He regarded her intently.

'Are you like your father, whom I never actually met? I mean recognisably so?'

'I don't think so. He was prematurely grey, a rather austere face.' Clive gave her an odd glance, but she was not looking at him, she was visualising her father's appearance, the clean-cut features, and well set head. He had been handsome enough to cause hearts to flutter among his female admirers, but engrossed in his work he never noticed them. Her mother might complain of his long absences, but she had no reason to suspect infidelity. 'I think all that was alike was our eyes,' she concluded. 'Why, does it matter?'

'Not at all,' Clive told her hastily, seeming to recollect her present need. 'Now drink this.'

He picked up the glass and handed her the pills. Obediently she swallowed them.

Schooling his voice to gentleness, he bade her:

'Have a nice long sleep.'

She snuggled down into her pillows. 'Oh, I will, but you—what will you do, Clive?'

'I'll just have another look round.'

'You ... you won't go far?' Anxiety sounded in her voice.

He made an impatient gesture, then restrained himself. 'No, I won't go far.'

Reassured, she closed her eyes. 'Thank you for everything.'

He made no response, turning away from her to look across the valley towards the Buddha. For centuries the image had stood there smiling down upon the absurdities of mankind, indifferent to their puny passions. Clive turned from that example of divine detachment and looked at the sleeping girl, her black hair sprayed on the pillow, her long lashes shadowing her cheeks. He gave a long sigh and went quietly out of the room. But the expression on his face when he looked at Angela had been inimical.

Angela woke from a long sedated sleep feeling refreshed and invigorated. She lay for a while going over her new-found memories. She had always known intuitively that her father had been with her on that plane, she decided, and that was why she had shrunk from facing the fact of his loss. The long snowbound weeks of oblivion had deadened the pain of her grief, which would have been much sharper if she had not been subconsciously prepared for the confirmation of his death. She had had too many blows in quick succession—her mother's decease, Arthur's desertion and then the crash. Nature had done her best for her by dropping a veil between her and her memories, until she was strong enough to resist the shock, and she had wilfully sought to perpetuate it. As Clive had told her, she had not wanted to lift it. Now that she had recollected everything, there would be no need for Clive's psychiatrist.

But where was Clive? It was growing dark, so she must have slept for a long time. While she made a hasty toilet—the hotel facilities were not very adequate —she examined curiously her girlish infatuation for Arthur, for she knew now that that was all it had been, wondering at its intensity. Her feeling for him was as dead as the dodo, and she was thankful it could have no aftermath. It would have been devastating to discover she was still engaged to him.

Angela went downstairs and found her husband had linked up with a party of German tourists, hearty red-faced men, who were downing potations which certainly were not tea with many 'Prosits', and much bonhomie. She was a little surprised, for Clive did not usually seek such company, at least as far as she knew he did not, but she realised anew how little she really knew him.

She stood in the doorway of what passed for a lounge, observing him, noticing how clear-cut and aristocratic his features were, how slim and lithe his figure compared with his companions' stocky forms and blunt faces. He wore, as they did, an open shirt and slacks, but even in that casual garb he contrived to look elegant. Her heart swelled with love and gratitude as she watched him. Where would she be but for him? If she had survived, she would probably be existing half demented among the Nuristani, unable to give an account of herself and accorded the veneration they extended to crazy people as the smitten by God. She knew she had been on the verge of losing her mind altogether, and only his patience and care had saved her sanity. Care, which he would have given to any pathetic creature that had needed it, and which had found its final expression in their marriage. But that, she thought sadly, was all that had motivated him; his desire for her body was ... merely desire. In all essentials they were actually complete strangers, and that was a poor foundation for a lasting union.

Since their arrival in Kabul, he had become an enigma to her. The bearded doctor in the Hindu Kush had been something of a paternal figure and she had thought she understood him; but he bore little resemblance to the clean-shaven man who had emerged from the cocoon of his winter garb upon their first morning at the hotel. She sensed Clive Stratton was far more complex than she had imagined, there were so many different facets to him, the doctor, the author

and explorer, Jasmine's husband, and latterly her own
lover, if she could call him that who never spoke of
love except with contempt as a youthful fantasy.

Clive looked up and saw her, hovering in the doorway.

'Hullo, woken up, have you?' he called cheerfully.
'Come and have a drink. Gentlemen, my wife.'

She went forward recalling almost with surprise that
she really was his wife. Ann Sullivan had ceased to
be.

The other men seemed to be a little embarrassed by
her appearance; they had not expected to find a
woman staying in the hotel. They were not, they explained in German, which she could not understand,
suitably clad for a lady's company. Clive laughed at
their punctiliousness and invited them to join them
for dinner.

Angela was sorry that he had done that. She was
eager to talk about her recently discovered past. Gradually it was borne in upon her that that was exactly
what her husband did not wish her to do. During the
meal she occasionally caught his eyes upon her with a
strange expression, almost as though he disliked her.
She dismissed the impression as her fancy. She was in a
hyper-sensitive condition and liable to misread the
most innocent glances.

To her disappointment, Clive arranged with his
guests to explore the valley by moonlight. The Buddha, they agreed, would look fantastic by night, and
there was an ancient stairway going up into its giant
head, from which there would be a remarkable view.

'You don't mind, Angela, do you?' Clive asked perfunctorily. 'It'll be too rough walking for you, and the
staircase is no doubt pretty rotten.'

'You'll take care?' she asked anxiously.

'I'm not a rash boy,' he rebuked her, with an impatient frown. 'You'd better get all the rest you can before our journey back tomorrow.'

She forbore to mention that she had been resting all the afternoon. Evidently this was to be a men's expedition, and they meant to go fast and far, so she had no choice but to agree, for as she had told him before their marriage, she meant never to be an encumbrance when he wanted to explore.

But not at Bamian, she thought, as she sat in her bedroom window watching their figures diminish with the distance as they crossed the valley, and not tonight of all nights. Uneasily she wondered if her return to normalcy had broken her hold over Clive. Possibly he preferred her to be the nameless waif whom he had succoured. It was a disquieting idea. Then she remembered that he had proposed to have her psychoanalysed, and dismissed it as another figment of excited fancy.

Unhappily she went to bed, longing for her husband's return, but though she lay awake for a long time, he did not appear. Very late, or rather early, she heard sounds of carousal downstairs. He must be whooping it up with his new acquaintances, but that again was uncharacteristic of Clive. She decided that he had been starved of male companionship, for the Nuristani were more specimens to be studied than congenial friends, and being Moslems they did not drink. She supposed that was what was attractive about the brash Germans; men seemed to have an incomprehensible urge to drink together. She finally fell asleep to the distant strains of *Deutschland über Alles.*

During the long drive back, she could not kid herself that there was not a distinct atmosphere. Clive was aloof and withdrawn. He made comments about the country through which they were passing, but half his mind seemed to be elsewhere. At last in desperation she enquired:

'What's wrong, Clive? I thought you wanted me to recover my memory. Now you seem displeased.'

'Of course I'm not,' he said quickly. 'It's not that.' He hesitated. 'Those fellows last night made me feel restless.'

Her heart sank.

'Regretting your bachelor freedom?' She tried to speak lightly.

'The wilderness presents no problems except survival,' he observed cryptically. 'That's one of its great advantages. But I really must go home.'

She sensed conflict between inclination and duty, and wished he would be more open with her. Surely as his wife she was entitled to his confidence? But Clive was a man who would always make his own decisions without consulting others, and perhaps he feared to hurt her feelings by confessing he was desirous of leaving her.

He did then make an effort, and it was an obvious effort, to interest himself in her affairs. He asked if she had any near relatives whom she would like to contact when she reached England. She shook her head:

'Daddy was an only child and his parents were dead. I have some aunts and uncles on Mother's side, but we didn't have much to do with them.'

They had deplored their sister's continual complaints, and had not been helpful during her last illness, being engrossed in their own families. Since Angela had nothing else to do, she was adequate to cope. Also she had found they were critical of her father for being so much away, but since his work took him far afield he could not be blamed for that. Any aspersion on her beloved father instantly roused Angela in his defence, and her hot words had not endeared her to her relations.

'They'll have been told I was killed in the crash with Daddy,' she went on. 'I don't think I'll bother to let them know I survived, at least, not yet.'

She would also have to tell them she was married, and she did not want to have to inform them of that. They would be altogether too inquisitive.

Clive seemed relieved by her decision, and he said compassionately:

'You do seem alone in the word, my poor waif, and I'm afraid I haven't much to offer you by way of a family either.'

'All I want is you,' she told him, her heart in her eyes.

But he was watching the road and at the fervour in her voice he looked faintly embarrassed.

'Thank you, dear,' he said perfunctorily. 'There's just one thing ...' He hesitated.

'Yes, Clive?'

'I don't like saying this, but it would be as well if you don't mention your maiden name to my people. Mother once knew some Sullivans whom she disliked intensely. It might prejudice her against you.'

She stared at his profile wide-eyed. 'How could it? You sound as if you thought my father had been a criminal, Clive!'

'Of course I'm not suggesting anything of the sort. It's just ... you know how unreasonable women can be about unimportant details.'

She felt vaguely disturbed, as if she had been asked to deny her father, but because she was always anxious to please Clive, she told him:

'It seems quite absurd to me, but if you wish it, I won't ever mention poor Daddy, nor our name, but please understand that I'm proud to be his daughter.'

'Naturally. It's only that the name has unpleasant associations for Celia.'

With a gleam of humour, she remarked:

'And it's going to be difficult enough to persuade her to accept a poor waif without such an unfortunate label.'

'Oh, she'll take to you all right,' he said without conviction.

'Do we have to live with her?'

'No. If she doesn't want to leave Abbotswood, we'll get another house, all that's got to be arranged when I get back. Of course it would be splendid if you manage to hit it off with Mother, you wouldn't be lonely then if I want to go away.'

'But I thought . . .' She checked herself. She had told him that she would not try to keep him from his exploratory adventures, but she had not expected he would want to go so soon, and he had talked about settling down. Was he going to dump her at this place in Dorset, and wash his hands of her?

He said with careful casualness: 'Hans Klaus is planning an expedition into the Bolivian jungle. It sounded rather fun.'

Hans had been one of the German party at Bamian. So this was what they had been hatching when he had sat up half the night with them. She tried to fight an increasing sense of desolation. Clive had rescued her, married her, and was already tired of her.

'You must go if you want to do so,' she said stonily.

'It was just a thought, but I doubt if I can get away.'

That statement gave her some comfort. It was a pity they had gone to Bamian and met the young men who

101

had so unsettled him, perhaps a pity too that she had discovered her identity. She had a curious impression that both happenings were linked.

They reached Kabul in time for dinner, and Angela found to her relief that Mrs Newcome had moved on. Clive, however, seemed to regret her.

'She was quite amusing company,' he observed.

'And you don't find mine exactly scintillating?' she said a little bitterly.

'Comparisons are odious,' he quoted. 'You're bright enough at times, but tonight you look very tired. You'd better go to bed early.'

She was very sleepy, having slept so badly the night before.

'Aren't you coming up?'

'I've various things to do first, before our early start tomorrow, and I think it might be as well to call upon the Consul and tell him we've discovered who you are. He may keep me very late.'

She had the impression that he was making excuses to avoid being alone with her. Something was very wrong, and she determined to demand an explanation when he came to bed, but she was very tired and she was sound asleep long before he returned. That he did come back was evident from his rumpled bed, but he was up and had gone downstairs when the waiter brought her her tea, and over breakfast he was so withdrawn and taciturn, she decided to let the matter rest. She concluded that he was resenting his lost freedom and the necessity to return home. There could be no other reason, and once he became reconciled to the inevitable he would become his old pleasant self again. Grown men, she thought indulgently, could be very like small boys when they were thwarted and had to do what they did not want to do.

CHAPTER SIX

WHEN Angela saw Abbotswood, she wondered how Clive could be reluctant to return to it, could have borne to tear himself away from it. It was a possession of which any man would be proud, and it had sheltered generations of Strattons.

The house was situated in a valley above a winding stream between the steep pointed hills that lie to the north of Sherborne. For those who had the energy to climb the saddle between the two peaks behind it was the reward of a magnificent view over Somerset to the Severn Estuary, the greens, browns and reds of the farm land melting into a horizon of tender blue and mauve, with none of the harsh stark outlines that had characterised the mountains round Kabul.

The interior was gracious, with high-ceilinged airy rooms and big windows, the furniture old and solid with a profusion of polished wood. It was a house that had been loved and cared for, and breathed an atmosphere of home.

Angela and Clive travelled down from London by rail and were met at Sherborne station by Ralph Stratton. Some eleven or so years younger than his half-brother, he was lean, dark, and vivacious. A butterfly where girls were concerned, he had not yet formed a serious attachment.

He was standing on the platform as their train came in, and as soon as Clive alighted from their compartment, he bore down upon him with a whoop of glee, slapping him on the shoulder.

'Welcome home, wanderer!' he exclaimed dramatic-
ally. 'And I hope you've come to stay. Ma can't manage
without one of us and it's my turn to spread my wings.'

'That so?' Clive enquired without enthusiasm.
'We'll go into all that later.' He looked disparagingly
at Ralph's costume, very full trousers in two colours, a
flamboyant shirt, and a fringed suede jacket. 'Aren't
you getting a little old for fancy dress?'

'It's never too old to be with it,' Ralph returned,
'and we've grown out of the pukka sahib stuff while
you've been away.'

Clive turned to Angela, who was watching this exchange with amusement. 'Angela, this ruffian is my
young brother. Ralph, meet your new sister-in-law.'

Ralph struck an attitude of rapt appraisal.

'Gorgeous!' he pronounced. 'You know how to pick
'em, Clive. Where did you find her? Your cable got us
all guessing. She looks as though she came out of a
Persian garden, but you're not a native, are you, love?'

'Certainly not,' she told him, laughing. 'I'm as Eng
lish as you are.'

Clive went to collect their luggage leaving the two
younger people staring at each other. Ralph was very
unlike Clive except for his clear grey eyes, which contrasted with his dark hair, but he was only his half-
brother. Actually he had arrived when his parents had
all but despaired of having any more children, and
one of their own.

'I don't know whether that's a relief or a disappointment,' Ralph told her. 'I was half hoping to meet an
Afghan houri or a Chinese geisha—sorry, my mistake,
geishas are Japanese, but it's better for the succession
that you're English. The village might jib at a foreign
squiress.'

Angela blushed. She had not discussed the possibility of a family with Clive, and she had no idea how he regarded it. Now it occurred to her that he might want a son to inherit Abbotswood, and, cheering thought, that might keep him at home.

'But you still haven't said where he found you,' Ralph rattled on, eyeing the outfit Clive had bought for her on their way through London. It was very simple, a plain blue dress and jacket, but it was beautifully cut. 'You look more like Paris than Kabul.'

Clive arrived with a porter in time to overhear his question.

'Her father was on a dig in Persia,' he said casually, a true but misleading explanation. 'And when I first met her, she didn't look like she does now.' He grinned at the recollection. 'This is my handiwork.' He touched his wife's shoulder possessively.

'You've made a good job of her,' Ralph conceded, 'though you couldn't have done it if she hadn't given you a good start. Let's get going. Poor Ma is expecting something out of the Arabian Nights,' he smiled wickedly. 'So we must hurry up and put her out of her suspense. You're a bit unpredictable, big brother. She was staggered when you cabled that you were bringing home a wife.'

Clive shot him a keen look. 'Why not?' he asked laconically.

'Exactly, why not? She can't expect you to remain the bereaved widower for ever. I'm all for it.' He glanced again at Angela. 'It'll be fun to have someone young about the place, and you look very young. What did you say your name was?'

'Angela,' she told him firmly.

'Angelic Angela, how apt.' He looked speculatively at his half-brother. 'But I didn't expect you'd descend to cradle-snatching, Clive.'

'I'm twenty-one,' Angela said stiffly, 'and I prefer mature men. Clive is in the prime of life.'

'Oh, quite. No doubt I spoke out of turn.'

'You did,' Clive told him repressively.

'But you know what Ma'll say,' the irrepressible one went on gaily as they reached the car.

'I hope she won't be so tactless,' Clive said sharply.

'I daresay she'll only think it,' Ralph observed airily.

'What?' Angela demanded.

'Never mind,' Clive bade her, and busied himself storing their luggage in the boot. Ralph opened the passenger door for Angela and she murmured as she stepped inside:

'What will your mother think? You'd better tell me.'

With half an eye on Clive, Ralph whispered:

'There's no fool like an old fool.'

'Oh!' Angela subsided on to the seat. 'But he isn't old, Ralph!'

'No, only old enough to know better, according to Mum, but I applaud his taste. Don't worry, Angela, I'll stand by you.'

'I'm not worrying,' she insisted bravely, but she quailed at the thought of meeting Mrs Stratton.

Clive came to claim the driver's seat, and Ralph got into the back.

'Thus do I relinquish the reins of government,' he announced.

'You can drive if you want to,' Clive told him ungraciously.

'No, no, it's your privilege, your car and your house. I was only the deputy.'

'Maybe I'll be asking you to deputise again,' Clive remarked as they drove out into the country without passing through the town.

'Oh no, you won't, not now you've got a wife. You're

going to become the lord of the Manor and rear progeny to carry on the name of Stratton. I'm going to London to make my fortune.'

Angela stole a look at Clive to see how he accepted this programme. She could only see his profile and his eyes were intent upon the road, but she noticed his jaw was set, and sensed that Ralph's remarks had not pleased him. His brother had obviously got his own plans which did not include continuing as a stand-in for Clive. Would that preclude his half-formed plans to go to Bolivia? Desperately she hoped it would.

The green of the trees and grass was refreshing after the barren heights of Afghanistan. Hawthorn bloomed in the hedgerows and lilac in the cottage gardens. She looked at the low emerald slopes of the hills as they entered the valley leading up to Abbotswood. She had never realised before what a beautiful and restful colour green was. The English countryside looked small, enclosed and safe after the savage grandeur of the landscapes she had been among for so long. She was happy to see it again, but she supposed it was too tame for Clive's adventurous spirit.

Mrs Stratton came to the door to meet them as the car drew up before the stone porch with its two pillars on either side, and three steps leading up to the front door of Abbotswood. She was a tall, dark, handsome woman with hair so intensely black, Angela suspected it was tinted to conceal the encroaching grey. Ralph bore some resemblance to her, Clive none at all, but Clive was not her son. He embraced her fondly, then stepped back to present his wife.

'This is Angela, Mother.'

Angela saw then with surprise that Mrs Stratton's eyes were blue, contrasting with her dark colouring, and they were hard as stones. She stared critically at the girl and Angela raised her own dark head defiantly. She knew in those first few moments of meeting that she was confronting an enemy. Celia Stratton resented Clive's second wife and there was open hostility in her gaze.

'Come in, dear,' she said, but with no warmth in her voice. 'Tea is ready, or would you like to go to your room first?'

'I would like a wash,' Angela admitted. 'Railway trains are so grimy.'

'Come upstairs, then, the boys will bring in the baggage.' Angela realised that though both men were grown, they would always be the boys to Celia.

She followed her up the broad carpeted stairs, along a passage and into a big bedroom. It was furnished with a double bed, a large wardrobe and a triple-mirrored dressing table. A door connected it with a dressing room containing another bed.

'I hope you'll be comfortable,' Celia Stratton said conventionally. 'The bathroom is next door with your towels. We have two. Ralph and I will use the other one.' Then she seemed to recollect something. 'But of course you'll be mistress here now and can make any changes that you wish.'

'I ... I wouldn't want to displace you,' Angela stammered awkwardly. 'It'll take me some time, a long time to ... er ... get used to everything.'

'Perhaps you've never lived in a country house?'

'No. We had a flat in London.'

'Very different. No space; we've plenty of that here, and naturally the housekeeping is very much more difficult. No running out to the supermarket whenever something's been forgotten.'

Angela wondered with dismay if Clive would expect her to tackle it, but not while his mother was still in the house. For the first time she was glad of Celia's presence.

Clive came in carrying their suitcases. He glanced round the room and then at Celia.

'We don't want to turn you out, Mother,' he told her. 'The guest room would have done for us.'

'The master and mistress should occupy the master bedroom,' she returned emphatically. 'I'm only the dowager now. I'll be quite happy in Jassy's old room.'

'But . . .' Clive looked worried.

'I prefer it,' she interrupted him. 'There I can be with my cherished memories. I've had her portrait moved in there.' Clive gave an exclamation of annoyance, and his stepmother's look was full of reproach. 'We haven't all forgotten Jasmine,' she said sadly. She turned to Angela. 'Wives can be replaced, but daughters can't. I suppose you know Clive married my girl by my former marriage? It made us such a united family, for of course poor Jassy wasn't a Stratton until Clive made her one.' She sighed. 'I've never ceased to grieve for her, and no one can ever take her place.'

She gave Clive a meaning glance as if to imply that if he thought he had found a substitute, she would prove inadequate. Then she went out of the room, closing the door softly behind her.

Angela was stunned by this disclosure. She cast back in her mind to the occasion upon which Clive had described his family to her. He had mentioned that his father had married a widow with a baby daughter, but he had not said what had become of the child, nor had she noticed the omission. Had it been deliberate? And if so, why?

'I'm sorry about that,' Clive said abruptly. 'You'd think that after nine years she'd let it rest.' He passed his hand wearily over his forehead, pushing up his fair forelock.

'You didn't tell me you'd married your stepmother's daughter,' Angela said reproachfully, realising that Clive and Jasmine must have been brought up together and by marriage she had gained his name, which was the only difference between her and Clive's father's children. A united family they had been in all truth. She felt terribly conscious of being an usurper in their compact circle.

'Didn't I? But I'm sure I told you Celia had an infant before she married Dad.'

'Yes, but you didn't mention that she grew up and became your wife.'

'Does that make any difference?'

'It does, because it accounts for Mrs Stratton's antagonism. You might have warned me.'

'Why, what could you have done?'

She thought about it. He was right. Pre-knowledge would not have changed anything, only increased her apprehensions.

Clive was pacing up and down the room with impatient strides.

'It's morbid,' he burst out. 'She makes a fetish out of her memories. Jassy's room, and that damned daub to stare at every night.' He stopped and gave Angela a quizzical look. 'It's a horrible painting and I wanted to burn it, but she wouldn't let me.'

'Of course she'd want to keep it,' Angela exclaimed. 'Even if it isn't very good.'

'You haven't seen it,' he returned with an enigmatical smile. 'But you will, she'll insist upon showing it to you, but it's not the sort of memento a man would want to keep of his wife.' He resumed his restless perambulations. 'It's unhealthy, this brooding over the past. Why can't she put it behind her? It isn't as if

Jassy had been her only child—she's got Ralph.'

Angela walked to the window and looked out. The house was situated a little way up a hillside so that the garden sloped to the brook that meandered along the valley floor. The beds were bright with spring flowers surrounding a terraced lawn enclosed by a red brick wall. Beyond was a shrubbery a mass of flowering trees, lilacs, rhododendrons, and laburnum. It looked too fair a place to be haunted by past sorrows. Clive's attitude was typically masculine, she thought, he wanted to bury his grief, but Celia being a woman cherished her memories. She said:

'She may have cared deeply for her first husband and her girl was all she had left of him. Then she lost her too. It was cruel luck, Clive.'

'Jasmine needn't have died,' Clive declared vehemently. 'It was her own folly . . .'

Angela turned round to look at him. He had sat down upon one of the beds, his head in his hands and his face was set in bitter lines.

'You mean . . . it was an accident?' she faltered.

He gave her a wary glance. 'Sort of,' he said. He stared at her inimically, almost as if she had been in some way responsible for Jasmine's death.

'Don't look at me like that,' she cried in distress. 'I haven't done anything.'

'No,' he said harshly. '*You* haven't.'

She stared at him questioningly and with an effort he brought himself back from his voyage among painful memories. His face cleared and he smiled at her.

'This is no way to welcome you,' he said apologetically. 'And it was all over and done with long ago. Poor Mother broods too much about the past. Perhaps now I'm come home to take over, I can persuade her to go away. A world cruise might reorientate her.' He stood up. 'I've been selfish, I've left her too much alone.'

'She had Ralph.'

'Just what I thought, but apparently he isn't enough —but I'm forgetting tea is waiting for us. Are you ready to go down?'

'No, I want to wash my hands. I won't be a minute.'

Angela hurried into the bathroom.

Celia presided over the silver tea-pot after ostentatiously offering that privilege to Angela, who hastily declined it. The sitting room was under Angela's bedroom and commanded the same view. French windows opened on to a terraced lawn surrounded by flower beds, a rockery connected it with a rose garden and below that was a shrubbery full of flowering bushes. Around the window, starred jasmine climbed the walls, and its scent permeated the room, a perpetual reminder of the girl who had borne that name.

Angela sat in an easy chair facing the window, Ralph lounged in another one, except when he sprang up to pass sandwiches, cake, and cups of tea. Clive sat beside his stepmother on the sofa and they talked of what had happened in the vicinity during his absence, and how the farm was progressing. Ralph watched them with amusement and threw occasional remarks to Angela. She was not responsive, for she was hurt by Clive's neglect. He seemed to be deliberately excluding her.

Tea over, he went off with Celia to look at some improvements in his domain, leaving Angela without excuse or apology. Ralph looked at her humorously.

'Like to look over the estate?' he asked. 'I'll take you, since Ma has monopolised Clive.'

'Thanks very much, but I think I'll wait until he's free to show me round.'

'Maybe you'll wait a long time,' he told her, a little

piqued by her rejection of his offer.

'I don't think so. Of course Mrs Stratton has a lot to tell him since he's been away so long,' she said in Clive's defence.

Ralph's expression became commiserating.

'You'll have to stick up for yourself,' he warned her. 'Otherwise Ma'll continue to monopolise him.'

'Oh, I shall,' she declared, and meant it, but she would choose her time to assert herself. 'I'd better go and unpack. Do you dress for dinner?'

'We spruce ourselves up a bit. Put on suits. Beastly bore, but Ma insists. She always changes her dress.'

Angela stowed her things and Clive's away in wardrobe and drawers with a feeling of impermanence. It did not seem possible that she was going to live in this beautiful house for months and years. She was more like an obligatory guest, and not a very welcome one at that. She had added to her clothes during their brief stop in London under Clive's directions. She had bought unwillingly, for she did not enjoy spending his money, but she realised he expected her to dress well to uphold his position. She wondered if her father had left anything; even a pittance of her own would enhance her self-respect. She would make discreet enquiries once she was settled, if she ever were settled in this hostile atmosphere. She could not quite explain her reluctance to accept Clive's bounty. It was normal for a husband to pay for his wife's clothes, unless she had her own money. It was partly because she was giving him so little in exchange; even his desire for her seemed to have died, and he did not need her to run his house. His stepmother was doing that much more efficiently than she could.

For dinner she put on a demure crimplene dress with short sleeves and a square neckline. Celia appeared in black chiffon with diamonds on her fingers and in her ears. Angela wondered which husband had been the donor. The two men wore dark suits. The meal was simple but excellently cooked and served.

'I'm training a local girl,' Celia announced, 'but I know as soon as she's proficient she'll go off to a town and leave me. They all do, though I pay a comparable wage. The lure of the bright lights.' She shrugged her shoulders. 'The sweet I prepared myself.' She glanced at Angela. 'Can you cook?'

'Just plain dishes,' Angela told her. She had been shown the kitchen, a vast apartment with a granite floor and single hearthrug as was common in those parts. The stove was a large Aga which also heated the water. She could not imagine herself preparing food upon that expanse of stove, she was used to a gas cooker. She told them so. 'But I expect I can learn,' she said hopefully.

'No need, unless you're in a hurry to make changes.' Celia gave her a barbed look.

'I'm not, but I think I should do something to justify my existence.'

'Good lord, how frightfully worthy,' Ralph laughed. 'I wouldn't dream of doing anything if I could find someone to do it for me—except amuse myself, of course.'

'That's what I want Angela to do,' Clive interpolated. 'She's had rather a hard time.' Celia looked at him interrogatively, but he did not elucidate. 'Just rest and lounge about, Angela, until you get ... er ... the feel of things. There's a swimming pool at the back of the house and a tennis court, and of course you ride.'

Angela knew he was referring to her expedition on muleback. She felt a wave of nostalgia for those happy carefree days when she had been just a nameless waif.

'Elephants or camels?' Ralph asked facetiously.

'My last mount was a mule,' Angela told him.

'Good heavens, only one degree better than a jack-ass!'

'It was the only beast that could keep its footing in the country we were traversing,' Angela explained with one eye on Clive.

'Oh, on your dig, I suppose,' Ralph suggested. 'Was Clive there, and did he ride a mule?' He looked audaciously at his half-brother.

'I preferred to walk,' Clive returned, refusing to be drawn.

Celia said dreamily: 'Jasmine was a wonderful horse-woman.'

Nobody made any comment; she had effectively closed the conversation.

Later, on their way back to the sitting room, Angela found Ralph beside her.

'The bitchiness of women!' he muttered. 'Ma hasn't mentioned Jassy for years. Now I suppose we'll have her dished up for breakfast, lunch, and dinner, unless Clive can muzzle her.'

'I hope so,' Angela said in dismay. If Celia were going to throw Jasmine up at her at every opportunity it would be more than she could bear.

Ralph invited Clive to accompany him down to the pub, declaring that the local inn was the best place to catch up with the gossip of the neighbourhood, and there he would meet several of his old cronies. Clive agreed with alacrity.

'Don't wait up for me,' he told Angela. 'You'll be tired after your journey.'

'I'm not all tired,' she flashed explosively, resenting this well-worn pretext to be rid of her. 'I'm pretty tough, as you should know. Can't I come with you?'

Celia clicked her tongue. 'Ladies don't go to pubs.'

'Perhaps they didn't in your day,' Angela was feeling exasperated, 'but you'll find plenty of girls in them now.'

'Another time,' Clive interposed. 'The local's only a rude sort of hostelry, Angela. I'll run you out to somewhere more exciting another time.'

Angela reflected that no English inn could be ruder than the tea-houses in Afghanistan, and she continued to look at Clive reproachfully.

Celia said indulgently: 'Let him go, Angela. He's dying for a masculine binge. The best of men, you know, can grow tired of feminine society.'

Angela flushed at the implied rebuke. She had no wish to try to keep Clive on strings, but as it was her first night in a strange place she thought he might have stayed with her. She made no further protest and the half-brothers went off like truant schoolboys.

'Brides have such a lot to learn,' Celia murmured with false sweetness.

'I think I'll go upstairs,' Angela informed her, unable to endure further baiting. 'I ... I haven't finished unpacking.' She had to offer some excuse out of politeness.

'Just as you like, my dear,' Celia cooed. 'I'll come up too. I'm a bit fagged. I had to get up very early this morning—such a lot to do, you know, and Ralph's so lazy. Someone has to see that the men arrive on time at the farm, but of course Clive will take over now.'

They walked upstairs together. Celia's door came first, and as she opened it, she said:

'Come inside, there's something I'd like to show you.'

Somewhat reluctantly Angela followed her inside. The room was not nearly so large as hers and the window looked sideways along the valley. The furniture was modern in light wood, the bed a divan with a rich golden brocade throw-over; an easy chair and a television set indicated that Celia also used it as a sitting room. A door into an inner closet was ajar, a space just big enough to make a dressing room. It contained a rug, a high chair, and a narrow polished table, its walls being painted severely in white. On the table was a silver bowl full of white roses, on either side of which was a three-branched candlestick, similar to those used upon altars, and above the table was a picture, the subject to whom this shrine was dedicated. Celia switched on a concealed light in the top of the frame, and Angela did not need to be told whom it represented. She was seeing Clive's 'damned daub.'

It was crudely painted, the colours too garish, but the artist had caught the erotic essence of his model, which perhaps was what Clive did not like. It was undoubtedly a beautiful face, the rich dark hair was loose, falling softly over bared creamy shoulders. Eyes, blue like her mother's, stared insolently out at the beholder, the full sensual mouth was curved in a little secret smile, the soft contours of cheeks and chin had a voluptuous warmth, belied by the hardness of the eyes. Lines from a poem once read long ago recurred to Angela.

> *Cold eyelids that hide like a jewel*
> *Hard eyes that grow soft for an hour;*
> *The heavy white limbs and the cruel*
> *Red mouth like a venomous flower;*

It was, she remembered, by Swinburne and she had been caught by the sensuous rhythm of the lines, and that was why they had stuck in her mind. 'Venomous

flower' was an apt description of those luscious lips—
and this was the girl who had been Clive's wife.

'My daughter, Jasmine,' Celia murmured beside her.
'Lovely, wasn't she? A man who once possessed her
would find every other woman insipid.'

Angela flinched, for Celia had put into words her
own increasing fear that Clive found her inadequate.
She studied Jasmine's pictured face avidly and felt an
increasing repulsion. Beautiful, yes, but it was an evil
beauty without the slightest hint of spirituality. Lilith,
perhaps, but never Eve, Lilith who had no soul. But
what man wanted spirituality? Women like Jasmine
could arouse and feed the hottest fires of amorous desire. She turned away from the sapphire eyes of the
portrait and the malicious gaze of the woman beside
her.

'Thank you for showing it to me,' she said coldly.
'I've got the message, but it's possible you may be
wrong. Clive isn't entirely sensual.'

Not the man who had tended her with such loving
care when she had been ill in both body and mind.
Instinctively she knew that there was a fineness in
Clive that could be repelled by Jasmine's blatant sex-
uality. Yet he had loved her, so perhaps the artist was at
fault, he had shown only one aspect of his sitter. She
did not know much about men. Arthur had been un-
complicated and not very demanding, rather conven-
tional in fact—perhaps that was what had been wrong,
they had been unable to wake passion in each other.
Her father had been austere and remote, bolstering up
a shaky union with a complaining wife. What fire had
once burned in him had sunk to ashes. There was fire
in Clive too that the lovely Jasmine had once ignited.
It was flared up once for herself, but now she had lost
the power to turn him on.

Celia's lips curled cynically. 'You're very naïve, aren't you, my girl? Clive's no Sir Galahad, but very human, and you, I fancy, must be frigid.'

Angela knew she was not that; perhaps it would have been better for her if she were.

'Goodnight, Mrs Stratton,' she said politely. 'I gather that is all you wanted to show me.'

'Isn't it enough?'

Angela looked straight into the malevolent eyes.

'It's only a portrait,' she pointed out, 'and the subject has been dead nine years, but I, Mrs Stratton, am very much alive and I shall fight to hold my own.'

'You've lost your battle before you've even begun it,' Celia told her. 'Clive tells me he's contemplating an expedition to Bolivia.'

Angela felt a constriction at her heart. He might have spared her that, but since he regarded this woman as his mother, she would receive all his confidences.

'He hasn't gone yet,' she said steadily. 'He may change his mind. Goodnight, Mrs Stratton.'

In her own room she felt lost and alone, her confidence ebbing. She longed desperately for Clive, but he did not come. She lay awake restless and miserable until dawn. Where was he, and what was he doing? He had declared that Jasmine's tragedy was over and done with. He had put years of roaming in far places between him and his loss, but he had never managed to forget her. Now he was home again his memories were catching up with him, and so he was contemplating another expedition. Jasmine was dead, but her presence still haunted Abbotswood; Clive knew that and that was why he wanted to flee from it. He had brought Angela back with him to help him to exorcise that restless spirit, but it was useless, he could not escape its influence.

119

A girl might be able to hold her own against another woman, but how could she contend with a glamorous ghost?

CHAPTER SEVEN

ANGELA showed no sign of the night's despair when she came down to breakfast, dressed for riding, for she had received a message with her early tea that she was to accompany the two men round the estate. Clive offered a vague apology for his desertion, explaining that they had decided to go fishing as it was such a lovely night; they had met a smack owner at the pub and driven down with him to the coast, whence they had put out to sea.

'In fact we're only just back,' he concluded.

Ralph looked a little wilted after a sleepless night, but Clive showed no sign of fatigue. The explanation was perfectly genuine, as the fresh mackerel cooked for breakfast proved. Angela scolded herself for being possessive, though she did say that Clive might have let her know he intended to be out all night.

'I didn't want to disturb anybody by ringing up, and I thought you'd be sound asleep,' he excused himself.

'Weren't worried, were you?' Ralph, who was more perceptive, enquired. 'I'm afraid we're very apt to do things on impulse and Clive forgot you aren't used to our ways. When something exciting turns up we leap at it, and Ma long since ceased to worry about us. You can't keep a Stratton on a leading rein.'

Precisely what she was thinking. The morning was so fresh and sunny that her heaviness of the night before disappeared. Celia did not come down to breakfast, Clive was attentive and Ralph amusing, so that she decided Abbtswood was a very good place to be in.

Down at the stables, Clive asked his brother to choose her a mount from among the half dozen riding horses.

'Something fairly docile,' he said. 'I've been away so long I don't know these beasts, and I don't want her to break her pretty neck.'

He gave Angela a glance which caused her heart to flutter. He was looking very attractive in yellow sweater, breeches and polished boots. When Ralph brought out a saddled horse, he lifted her on to its back with firm possessive hands. Her spirits rose as she looked down at him from that elevation and saw a flicker of flame in his eyes. He had not become indifferent, it was only the pressure of the events of the last few days that had kept him from her. Perhaps he really had believed she had been over-fatigued back in Kabul and had bridled his desires to let her rest. Tonight she would insist that she needed no further solicitude and triumph over the memory of that dark siren enshrined in his stepmother's ante-room. A gallop over the fields drove away any lingering apprehensions. It was good to be alive, to feel a swift horse under her, to have Clive in pursuit of her, for being of much lighter weight her mount outdistanced his. They returned in high spirits and Ralph complimented her upon her horsemanship.

'The mule must have been excellent practice,' he observed slyly, 'and if your tennis is equal to your riding, I'll have a job to beat you.'

'I haven't played tennis since I was at school, so I don't suppose I'll be in your class. Do you want to beat me?'

'Of course, to establish my male superiority, but if Clive partners you, you'll wipe the court with me.' He glanced admiringly at his half-brother. 'He's tops at everything, and he's played at Wimbledon.'

'That was in my salad days,' Clive interposed. 'I'm out of practice too, but I think I must go over the farm accounts this afternoon, if that's when you're thinking of playing.'

'I should have thought you could have taken a few days' holiday before you take over,' Ralph pointed out. 'Isn't this still your honeymoon?' Angela coloured and he laughed delightedly. 'Good lord, Clive, this wife of yours can still blush—what an enchanting phenomenon among our hardboiled lassies! If I went out to Persia, would I find another like her?'

'Most improbable. Angela's unique,' Clive told him, drawing his wife's arm through his. Words and action pleased her so much she felt capable of coping with the venom of a dozen stepmothers at lunch.

Mrs Stratton, however, seemed subdued. She contributed little to the lively banter between the younger ones. Ralph was expecting visitors that afternoon to play tennis, including a girl called Kathy.

'Who was my latest flame until you appeared,' he told Angela.

'Poor Kathy,' Angela laughed, 'but she'll know I can't be a serious rival.'

'Why not?' Celia Stratton's voice was harsh. 'This is a permissive age, and she wouldn't be the first Stratton bride to play the wanton.'

Angela stared at her, aware of sudden tension; she

glanced at Clive and saw his face was bleak. Ralph broke the constraint by saying:

'Wanton—what a delightfully old-fashioned word, Shakespearean, isn't it? Nowadays we use a Biblical one, but it doesn't apply to Angela. I'm quite sure she isn't permissive ... unfortunately.'

He looked so rueful that Angela had to laugh, while Clive had the self-satisfied look of a man who owns what other men desire. The awkward moment passed, but she was left with a query. Who was the unfaithful Stratton bride? Some cavalier ancestress in a notoriously promiscuous age, or someone nearer to hand to provoke Clive's grim look? Could it possibly have been Jasmine?

During the afternoon she forgot the incident in the turmoil of tennis. Kathy duly arrived with a brother in tow, a healthy, hearty young sportswoman, who claimed Ralph as her partner in spite of his obvious reluctance. She proceeded to make mincemeat of her opponents, although Ralph was only playing half-heartedly. Angela and her brother only won one game in the first set and it looked as if the second one was going to be love to the other side until Clive came on to the court.

'Score five games to nil,' Ralph called. 'Take Brian's racket, Clive, and give Angela a boost.'

'Oh, let's finish this set,' Kathy objected, anxious to win.

But Brian handed his racket to Clive to make what should have been his service. The four smashing balls Clive put down into the court won him a love game. Then Ralph seemed to rouse himself and the next was bitterly fought. Stimulated by the fast play, Angela found herself returning balls she would normally have missed or sent into the net. Kathy fought well and gamely to support Ralph's brilliant play, but they were not a match for Clive, even though Angela was not a great support to him. After she had taken the service, which mercifully she usually managed to return, he told her, 'Leave it to me.'

They retrieved the set and won it, to Kathy's chagrin.

'I'd no idea you were such a powerful player,' she said to Clive.

He grinned. 'I haven't played for years, didn't know I still could.'

'Old champions never die,' Ralph sang tunelessly. 'Clive and Jassy won the mixed doubles at Wimbledon one year, Kathy. She was even better than he was.'

'Jassy?' Kathy queried, then recollecting something she had been told, 'Oh, yes, of course,' and began to talk of something else.

For Angela the sunlight seemed suddenly clouded. She had enjoyed the game and admired Clive's proficiency. Standing by the net, still breathing a little fast from his exertions, his fair hair ruffled by the slight breeze, he looked almost a boy, the boy he had been when he had partnered Jassy. Angela had been proud of him and her small part in supporting him, then had come Ralph's careless words, uttered she was sure without thought. Jasmine had been a champion player, she had partnered Clive at Wimbledon in distant days, when Angela had been only a child. Had he recalled Jasmine when she had made blunders, her brilliance, her grace? He must have given up tennis when she had died, finding it too poignant a reminder of his loss; perhaps this was the first time he had played since, and the game must have recalled her.

'Gosh, what a clanger,' Ralph muttered beside her. 'Why can't I keep my tongue off that wench? I'm getting as bad as Ma!'

Kathy and Brian were talking eagerly to Clive; the girl too had Wimbledon aspirations and the disclosure that he had played there had excited her. That Clive was reluctant to speak about it did not deter her. Ralph watched them gloomily swinging his racket.

'You can't help it,' Angela told him. 'Jasmine's still here, you know, she haunts the place.'

'That's a bit far-fetched, honey.'

She shivered. 'I'm conscious of it if you're not. I suppose you were very fond of her too?'

'My dear girl, she was years older than me and she had no use for schoolboys. Actually I was away at college when she died. I don't know any details. Ma was devastated and Clive went away. I missed him a lot more than I did her. That marriage was a ghastly mistake, but Ma had it organised from the time they were infants. She wanted Jassy to be mistress here.' He wrinkled his dark brows. 'I don't think Jass was all that keen, she had other fish to fry.'

'But wasn't she in love with him?'

'I don't think Jassy was capable of loving anyone except herself, but neither of them would dream of confiding in me. Look out, the Wimbledon conclave is breaking up.' Clive was coming towards them. 'I shouldn't be deluging you with family history.' Ralph laid a hand upon her arm and added earnestly: 'But it *is* history, it was all over nearly ten years ago.'

Angela wished she could believe it was.

Since they were a quartet, they played Bridge after dinner. When Angela admitted she could not play, Celia insisted she must learn, Bridge was a social necessity; but Angela had no aptitude for cards, she bid wildly and could not remember which trumps were out. Clive who was her partner announced wryly that if they had been playing for money, she would have ruined him. Celia smiled with satisfaction, from which Angela deduced that Jasmine had been a skilful player and this was an attempt to humiliate her. However, it misfired, because the men ceased to take her efforts seriously and derived considerable amusement from her naïve blunders.

On their way to bed, Celia waylaid Clive. Some problem had arisen about which she must consult him. She favoured Angela with her hostile stare while she demanded her husband's presence. Angela went upstairs alone. Ralph had preceded them.

She undressed and showered, and put on the negligée which she had bought at Clive's instigation for her wedding night. The nightdress was in pale gold double nylon, the over-gown in apricot with golden frills. It fell about her in a froth of diaphanous drapery. Her long hair she brushed and left loose. She picked up the scent spray on her dressing table, and deluged herself in 'Evening in Paris' and hoped it was a perfume Clive liked. She heard Clive's voice in the passage, bidding his stepmother goodnight. She held her breath in anticipation listening for the sound of soft footfalls along the carpeted passage, willing him to knock upon her door. The footsteps went past, and she heard a door open and close, the one into his dressing room. There were vague sounds from within, and then he went into the bathroom. He was there some time, probably also taking a shower. Then he re-entered his dressing room; she wondered vaguely if the bed in it had been made up, she had a suspicion that it was, probably on Celia's orders. She waited, but there was no further sound from behind the door connecting their rooms. He was not coming to her, not even to say goodnight. She switched off her light and drew back the curtains from her window. It was a still, starlight night awaiting the rising of the waning moon, with falling dew. The garden scents invaded her nostrils— lilac, syringa, and ... jasmine. From a tree to the side of the house came the amorous moan of wood doves. A pair nested there and their intermittent cooing could be heard all night.

Angela's eyes went to the line of light under Clive's door. He was still awake, perhaps reading as he often did to compose his mind for sleep.

'A chapter of a dull book is an excellent soporific,' he had once told her.

She drew a deep breath, summoned up all her resolution and went to open the door. She turned the handle softly, dreading she might find it locked, and all that would imply. It was not. Quietly she opened it and stepped inside.

Clive was seated on the bed, a maroon silk robe covering his lean length. He was perusing a batch of papers which looked commercial and was making occasional notes on a pad, lying on the bedside table. The soft glow from the lamp also set upon it turned his hair to molten gold, and his smooth brown face to copper; there were as yet few lines upon it.

Angela stood silent, regarding him, until becoming aware of her presence, he looked up and saw her.

'Hullo, waif,' he said pleasantly. 'Anything wrong?'

'Everything's wrong,' she told him passionately. 'To start with, you haven't said goodnight.'

'How very remiss of me.' A wary look had come into his eyes at her tone, but he spoke lightly. Carefully putting his papers under the lamp, he stood up. 'Mother distracted me.' He brushed his hair back from his forehead, a familiar gesture. 'Goodnight, my dear.' He put his hands on her shoulders and gently touched her cheek with his lips. 'Sleep well.'

This dismissal, as if she were a tiresome child, was too much for her. Fiercely she cried:

'Oh, Clive, why are you so cold?' and flinging her arms about his neck she clung to him. 'I'm your wife,' she whispered into his neck. 'Not your sister.'

She felt a tremor run through his body. His arms closed round her automatically, his mouth sought hers. Triumph swelled in her breast; it had only needed a little audacity to win him back. His lips moved from hers to linger on her throat, her neck, and down towards her breast.

'Come to bed,' she whispered, and got no further, for he suddenly almost violently thrust her away from him. She saw the pupils of his eyes had expanded, turning the grey to black, and his nostrils quivered.

'Did you have to bathe yourself in scent?' he asked harshly. 'I loathe the stuff!'

So much for 'Evening in Paris'!

Astonished, bewildered, she stammered: 'I'm sorry, I ... I didn't know.'

He stood regarding her flowing drapery, her cloud of hair, and a spasm crossed his face. 'Are you trying to play Delilah?' he demanded. 'Those sort of tricks don't appeal to me. I like my women honest.'

'Yes ... no ... Clive, you're being horrible,' she cried childishly.

He passed his hand wearily over his eyes. 'I'm sorry, Angela—that scent has associations.'

She said with a flash of temper: 'I suppose Jasmine used it.'

He made no rejoinder, but turned away, absently rearranging the articles on the dressing table.

'Is it always like this with a second wife?' she went on bitterly. 'Perpetual reminders, comparisons? I know I can't compete with her, you're still obsessed by her, you should never have married again.'

He looked at her sombrely.

'I married you to give you a name,' he reminded her, 'and to get you out of Afghanistan.'

'And you expect me to be everlastingly grateful? But if that was all, why did you insist upon making it a real marriage?'

'Because I wanted you,' he said simply.

'Which you no longer do.' She paused, hoping he would deny her statement, but he said nothing. 'You should have had more foresight, Clive,' she continued accusingly. 'I ... I appreciate your chivalrous act, of course, but if you'd kept it a marriage in name only we could have got it dissolved when we were back in England. Now we'll have to wait ages before we can get a divorce.'

'Do you want a divorce?'

She did not, she wanted to cling to what little she had of him, even if she did have to share him with Jasmine. Words he had spoken returned to her. 'Most women have to share their husbands,' but in this case, Jasmine had taken the larger portion.

'Don't you?' she countered.

'No, I do not,' he told her unexpectedly. 'I know you're feeling sore, but the fact is ... No, I can't explain yet. But everything will come all right if you'll be patient, my dear. Give me a little time ...'

'Time for what?' she interrupted. 'To forget Jasmine? You can't, the whole place simply reeks of her, and Mrs Stratton does all she can to keep her memory alive.'

'That's why I'm considering living somewhere else.' He indicated the papers he had been perusing. 'Those are house agents' particulars. Away from Mother, we could make a fresh start.'

'But this is your home.'

'It hasn't been home for a long while. I used to love it.' He moved restlessly. 'But she poisoned it for me.'

She did not know if he meant Jasmine or his step-mother. Sitting down on the bed, she said sadly, 'What a pity, it's such a charming house.'

'So you like it? I thought you were a town girl.'

'We only lived in a town because it was more convenient for Daddy with so much coming and going, but he always hoped to retire into the country. He'd have loved Abbotswood.'

'Ah, yes, your father.' A peculiar expression came into his eyes, that she could not interpret. 'Almost I could wish that you'd remained a nameless waif.'

'You were anxious enough for me to regain my memory, and you ought to be pleased that I'm a famous archaeologist's daughter, when I might have been someone much less desirable for all we knew. Daddy was top-notch in his field, you know.'

'And you're very proud of him?'

'Of course I am.' She looked at him uncertainly, sensing some sort of antagonism. 'Oh, I wish you could have known him, I'm sure you would have got on well together, you'd have had a lot in common, for he was a wanderer too.'

Clive turned away with a harsh laugh. 'Yes, we had something in common.'

Puzzled by his attitude, she asked: 'Have you got something against archaeologists?'

'I don't like the breed.' He gave somewhat vague reasons. They had been known to smuggle out treasures that belonged to the countries where they were working, they neglected their families to pursue their mania.

Stung by such unjustifiable prejudice, she told him:

'The last could apply to you. Aren't you planning to go to Bolivia?'

'No. When it was suggested it seemed a solution to a problem, but I'm not sure it is now, and as Ralph's going to London, I'm needed here.'

Angela experienced a flood of relief. She had dreaded his departure, and though it was not flattering that she was not one of his reasons for staying, at least she would not be parted from him. As for the problem he mentioned, that must be Jasmine, though he would never solve that by continuing to run away. Since he was going to stay it was all the more important that she should break down the incomprehensible barrier that seemed to have risen between them. A possible explanation occurred to her.

'Has the discovery of my parentage put you against me?' she demanded. 'Surely you can't be so unfair and unreasonable?' He did not answer and she went on vehemently: 'Daddy was a fine man, an honest man, he'd never stoop to steal, and he didn't have much inducement to stay at home. Mother was forever ailing and nagging at him, but he always came back to her, when a more selfish man would have left her.'

'It's sometimes convenient to have a wife in the background,' Clive observed sarcastically.

Angela shook back her hair and stared at him defiantly.

'Look, has someone being telling lies about Daddy? If so I'd like to know, so I can refute them.'

'Your loyalty does you credit,' he said gently. 'Keep your illusions, child. Far be it from me to destroy them.'

'Then you have heard something?'

He shrugged his shoulders.

'Why should I?'

Dissatisfied, for she was sure he was being evasive, she told him: 'You shouldn't credit gossip, though I'm sure there could be none about Daddy.'

'I never heard any.'

'Well, then ...' She searched his unrevealing face and sighed. 'You're an enigma, Clive. Something has changed you and I don't know what it can be, unless,' her lips quivered—'you find me too young and childish and you're bored with me. I haven't any feminine wiles to entertain you.'

So great a contrast to Jasmine with her sexy lure.

'Thank God for that!' Clive exclaimed. 'Though I don't know what else this is.' He lightly touched her negligée, and smiled mockingly.

'It was bought to please you,' she reminded him.

'So it was, but an honest woman doesn't need frills and scent to keep her husband's ... respect,' he told her.

But it was not respect that she wanted, and she was sure he had substituted it for another word. She looked at him appealingly, but he would not meet her eyes.

'You'd better go to bed, little one,' he bade her.

Despondently she moved towards the door; the big master bedroom yawned emptily before her. The room Clive must have shared with his first wife. Celia knew what she was doing when she had insisted that they must occupy it. She turned round and saw that Clive was reaching for his papers again.

'I suppose the truth is you dislike my room because it was Jasmine's,' she said bitterly, 'and you can't bear to be with me in her bed.'

'It was never her bed,' he corrected her, 'she always had the room Mother's in now, nor did I ever sleep with her.'

'But ... but she was your wife ...' Astonished, she moved towards him.

'You may as well know the truth. She ran out on me on our wedding day.' He laughed at Angela's incredulous expression. 'You're jumping to conclusions, my waif. Technically she was my wife in that we went through the marriage ceremony, the empty vows which she never meant to keep and broke within the next twenty-four hours.'

He moved to the window and started to fiddle with the curtains, Angela sat down on the bed again, her eyes fixed expectantly upon his back.

'But why wait until the last minute?' she asked. 'It seems a lot of trouble for nothing.'

'It was a lot of trouble for nothing, but Jassy had always fancied a white wedding, and what Jassy fancied she got, with no thought to the trouble and pain she caused. Well, she had her fun, the whole county in attendance, me dressed up like a tailor's dummy, herself in white lace and satin, a train a mile long, a cake six feet high.' He leaned his head against the window frame and closed his eyes. Angela wanted to go to him, to draw his head down upon her breast, to comfort him for that past hurt, but it was not comfort from her he wanted, and besides, she wished to hear the rest of the story. He continued in sharp clipped sentences.

'We were going up to Scotland by motorail for the honeymoon after spending a night in London. At the reception she said she felt ill. She went up to her room and threw a fit of hysterics. Mother gave her a sedative, told us she wasn't fit to travel. That was a damper on the proceedings. I felt an utter fool. We got rid of the guests somehow. Mother told me I mustn't disturb ... my bride. She had had a brainstorm, but she was sure she'd be all right next day after a good sleep. We could cut the night in London and go straight up to Scotland. But in the morning, Jasmine had gone.'

'Oh, no!' Angela exclaimed.

She had followed his narrative intently, her imagination filling in the details. She could visualise the glamorous Jasmine sweeping up the aisle—she must have looked superb—to where a younger Clive awaited her immaculate in morning dress, his eager eyes alight as they feasted on his bride's beauty. It was the sort of scene that was the climax of a young girl's romantic dreams, for even sophisticated modern youth still yearns for white satin and a church spectacle, with her man waiting for her by a flower-decked altar. Clive would have represented every girl's ideal, young, ardent and handsome. What a pair he and Jasmine must have made, but Jasmine had fled from him.

'Why?' she asked blankly.

Turning from the window, Clive said sardonically:

'Because what none of us realised was that Jasmine was only attracted by the unobtainable. Mother had always planned that she should marry me. She wanted to see Jasmine mistress of Abbotswood when my father went, and that was always understood while Jassy and I were growing up, but she was so sure of me that I lost any appeal I might once have had for her.' He smiled wryly and resumed:

'She was in London during my father's last illness— Mother considered a house containing an invalid too depressing for a young woman, and he wasn't her father. He was ill a long time before the end. Jassy had a whale of a time and ran heavily into debt, among other extravagances she put up a large sum towards an archaeological expedition to the Med.'

He paused, and Angela thought she saw a chink of

daylight. But it was unfair to censure an honourable profession because of the folly of a girl. She said defensively:

'But, Clive, that's not unusual. Big expeditions have to have sponsors, even students pay premiums for the privilege of being included.'

'Jasmine didn't care a hoot about excavations,' he returned. 'It was the personnel she was interested in. Well, Mother had to sort her out. I think she paid all her debts out of what my father left her on condition that Jasmine came home and married me. Naturally I didn't know anything about their bargain, I was delighted that Jasmine had returned to me. She ... she bewitched me, Angela,' he sounded almost apologetic, 'she was maddeningly alluring.'

'You needn't tell me that,' Angela commented bitterly. 'I've gathered that for myself.'

Clive did not seem to hear her, his eyes had an inward brooding look as he reviewed the past.

'She left a note when she, fled—a typical Jasmine touch. She stated that she'd enjoyed the wedding, it had been a good show—her description—I'll not forget it—but she'd decided she'd rather go on a dig than up to Scotland. Touring was a bit of a drag. No regret for leaving me in the lurch, no apology for the humiliation she had brought on the family, she might have been declining a casual invitation. We traced her to London Airport, but her flight had gone and that was the last we heard of her for some months.'

'You mean she came back?'

'Yes, when her lover had ditched her, for of course she'd gone with a man. He was a great deal older than herself and married. She told us offhandedly that he'd promised to divorce his wife if she would free herself, but he had changed his mind and gone back to his home. She declared she was well rid of him, he'd become a bore, but that was mere bravado. Her vanity, the biggest part of her, had taken a hard knock. Mother urged me to forgive her and take her back, and I was so besotted I believe I might have done, but before I could bring myself to pardon her, she was dead.'

'In an accident?'

'So the coroner decided. She'd gone down to the coast and hired a boat which capsized. She was drowned.'

'How dreadful!'

Clive looked at her with unseeing eyes. 'At the inquest it was discovered she was pregnant, but it couldn't have been my child.'

Angela gave a small sound of distress, and Clive laughed. 'Not a pretty story, is it? Only Mother and I knew that, of course, and poor Mother was demented. She put all the blame on the man for enticing Jasmine away from her duty. She wanted me to go after him and shoot him. A hundred and fifty years ago I might have called him out, but now we live in a more civilised society and this sort of irregularity is all too common. Nor did I consider Jasmine was worth committing murder for. So Mother had to content herself with demanding vengeance from heaven, and her imprecations were quite spine-chilling.'

'I suppose it relieved her feelings,' Angela said with a shiver. Mrs Stratton must have been awe-inspiring in her rage. 'At least it couldn't do anybody any harm.'

'I don't know about that,' Clive returned in an odd voice. 'The man was killed.'

'But that could only have been a coincidence,' Angela insisted. 'So you knew who he was?'

'Of course I did, but his name's best forgotten.'

136

Angela thought it was a pity Jasmine's could not be forgotten too, but her hold over Clive must have been very strong to have lasted for so many years.

'I'm glad you've told me all this,' she said. 'I'll feel more sympathetic towards Mrs Stratton now, though I don't see why she has to take it out on me. I've never harmed her, but I suppose she can't bear to have Jasmine supplanted.' She looked doubtfully at her husband. 'Perhaps now we've come back here, you feel the same way?'

'Don't talk rubbish,' he said brusquely, 'and I think you imagine much of Mother's hostility. So long as you don't . . .' he broke off and glanced at her warily.

Silence fell between them, while outside the moaning of the doves was clearly audible. Clive's gaze wandered over Angela's slight form clad in the filmy drapery put on to entice him, her long hair that he had liked to play with during her so brief period of happiness, her troubled dark eyes. His own eyes kindled, he made a movement towards her, and Angela's heart leaped, but before he could touch her, he checked himself and turned away.

'No,' he said firmly. 'There's something that has to be put right before . . .' again he broke off, and looked faintly embarrassed.

'Clive, what's the difficulty? Can't you tell me?' she urged eagerly.

He shook his head. 'It might distress you. I'll explain when I've made the necessary arrangements, but I'm sure it'll be all right eventually.'

'You mean . . . leaving here?' she hazarded.

'Not entirely.' He looked at her again, but now his glance was cold. 'Meanwhile, Angela, for God's sake don't try to play the seductress, you don't know what harm you're doing. Go to bed, it's very late.'

This abrupt dismissal chilled her, and she rose obediently to her feet. 'Goodnight, Clive,' she said wistfully.

'Goodnight, Angela,' he returned without looking at her.

Sadly she trailed into her own room. She was tired of mysteries and evasions, and the deduction she drew from Jasmine's story was that Clive was still entirely obsessed by his first wife. She put no reliance upon his vague assurance that their relationship would eventually be all right. Jasmine's influence was still paramount at Abbotswood, and if he were hoping a change of residence would break her spell, Angela thought he was deceiving himself. Jasmine would follow them wherever they went, and she herself was quite incapable of compensating for her loss.

CHAPTER EIGHT

IT was quite by chance that Angela noticed the advertisement. She was idly scanning the columns of a newspaper while she waited for Ralph to go riding, when her father's name caught her eye. It was one of those notices put out by solicitors appealing for next of kin who upon application would learn something to their advantage. Several times it had crossed her mind that Edmund Sullivan must have left something that should of right be hers and she had intended to make enquiries, when a suitable opportunity presented itself.

She made a note of the solicitors' address, the name

was not unfamiliar to her. Selwyn and Hampson had managed her father's affairs, and Mr Hampson was known to her. She would go and see him at once, for by good luck Ralph had asked her to go to London with him at the end of the week. He was being interviewed for a job and had declared it would be an excuse for a binge. Clive had raised no objection, merely remarking that he was sorry he was too busy to accompany them, and Angela was looking forward to the excursion. While Ralph kept his appointment, she could call upon the solicitors.

She had been hoping that she might find she had something of her own, however small, for it still irked her pride to be utterly dependent upon Clive for every penny, especially as all was not well between them. Mrs Stratton remained firmly enthroned as mistress of the house, and Angela continued to feel like a guest and one who could set no limit to her visit. Clive had said he was looking for another property, but seemed halfhearted in his efforts to find one. She suspected he was secretly loath to leave Abbotswood in spite of its memories, or could it be because of them?

Once when Mrs Stratton had gone into Sherborne and the men were out on the farm, Angela had crept into Celia's room for another look at Jasmine's portrait. To her excited fancy the jewel-hard eyes under their heavy lids had seemed to her to stare at her with insolent triumph. Her predecessor knew her influence could never be exorcised, she reached out from beyond the grave to clutch at the man she had wronged, but would never relinquish. Jasmine had been the type of woman who having once annexed a member of the opposite sex would expect to hold him in thrall for ever. Deprived of the one she wanted, she refused to loose her tentacles from the one who had wanted her.

Was the accident really suicide, or was that the measure of Clive's self-reproach because he had hesitated to forgive her desertion? Her self-love must have been deeply wounded by his hesitation and the chagrin caused by the imperviousness of the one man she had found was indispensable. Clive's attitude towards that unknown man, Angela thought, was unfair. It was to his credit that he had chosen to respect his marriage vows, and Jasmine had known he was not free and the risk she was taking. She too had made vows which she had promptly broken, so she was every bit as reprehensible as her lover. But Clive had been in love with Jasmine and her tragic end had given him a profound shock, so that however badly she had behaved, he naturally put all the blame upon her traducer and his name had become anathema in the Stratton household.

Angela shivered as she looked up at the glowing beauty that had wrought such a coil, and pitied her rival. Lovely, passionate and undisciplined, she had brought happiness to no one, least of all herself.

The sapphire eyes seemed to mock her compassion. 'Pity me, do you, nitwit?' she seemed to say. 'What do you know of the wild ecstasies I enjoyed? Wouldn't you give your right arm to be able to kindle in Clive the passion I did, and leave him eating his heart out for you, as he still is, even after nine long years.'

Even after nine long years. Angela went out of the room softly closing the door behind her. Clive's feeling for her had died in less than a week, it could not survive the poignancy of his memories. She fancied she could hear derisive laughter coming from behind the shut door. Truly Jasmine haunted Abbotswood.

Angela felt a lift of spirits on the Friday morning upon which she left for London with Ralph. They made an early start, for they were going by road, and Ralph was in a lively mood.

'It's a long way, perhaps we shan't get back tonight, in which case your reputation may be endangered, Mrs Stratton,' he said gaily. 'Do you think if that happens Clive will shoot me?'

Angela shuddered. Celia had wanted Clive to shoot another man, the one who had stolen Jasmine from him, which gave a sinister overtone to Ralph's light-hearted question, but she managed to return brightly:

'I'm sure he wouldn't want to waste his ammunition,' and added a little bitterly, 'He wouldn't care.'

'Oh, he would, but I'm sure he trusts you. You're not like Jassy. She was a bitch.'

Why did he have to mention Jasmine on this perfect morning, for it was a lovely day, when she had for once escaped the brooding presence in the old house? Perhaps he had telepathically caught her own thought. She told him that Clive had given her all the details of that sad story.

'He thinks she drowned herself on purpose,' she concluded.

'Stuff, Jass loved life too well to do that, of course it was an accident,' Ralph said reassuringly. 'She could always get herself another man if Clive wouldn't forgive her. She wasn't fussy.'

'But she must have really loved the one she ran away with, to ditch Clive on his wedding night.'

'Sheer perversity, if you ask me. Jass liked to be dramatic. You see, she wasn't all that gone on Clive, she knew him too well, and they say familiarity breeds contempt. Ma made a big mistake by persuading her into it, and it would please her twisted sense of humour to think of Clive defrauded at the last moment.'

'It was a cruel thing to do,' Angela said heatedly.

'Jass was cruel.'

'Oh well, you knew her, but can't we talk about something else?'

'Good idea. Don't know why I brought her up, she's best forgotten.'

Angela heartily agreed, but it seemed impossible to consign Jasmine to oblivion.

Ralph left her in the City and she wended her way through the busy streets to the solicitors' offices. She had met Mr Hampson socially, but she had never attended his place of business before. It was up a dark narrow alleyway, and the interior seemed dingy and dim after the brightness outside. She was asked to wait in a stuffy little anteroom, while a clerk reported her name and business. She thought he looked at her a little oddly and she wondered if there had been other claimants to her father's estate. Her mother's relations, she supposed, would be next in line and they would forget they had not liked her father if there were any money to be gained.

'Mr Hampson will see you now, Mrs Stratton.'

Angela got up and followed the clerk down a narrow passage, he opened a door at the end of it almost reverently and announced her name.

The silver-haired man behind the desk stood up.

'Good morning, Mrs Stratton, will you take a seat?' He indicated the chair in front of his desk, then re-seating himself, looked at a note on his pad. 'You've come about the late Mr Sullivan's estate ...' He paused, stared at her, took off his glasses, rubbed them and stared at her again as he put them on. 'Good lord, you can't be Ann Sullivan?'

'I was,' she corrected him. Then it struck her that he must believe she had been killed in the air crash. 'I ... I survived.'

Briefly she told him her story, while he gaped at her.

'A truly wonderful escape,' he commented when she had finished. 'And almost incredible. My dear young lady, I'm delighted that you survived. Of course I recognised you—I saw you at your mother's funeral and upon other occasions. You know I was a friend of your father's as well as his man of affairs. Why didn't you contact me before?'

Angela explained that she had intended to do so eventually, but had had so much else upon her mind. Getting married ... here she blushed charmingly, and settled in her new home, which was some distance from London.

'Of course,' the kindly brown eyes twinkled. 'Learning to be a new wife.' He referred to a file on his desk. 'Did you know that your father left a quite considerable sum of money?'

'You surprise me. I ... we never seemed to be well off.'

She remembered Clive's indictment, that archaeologists sold treasures on the side, but her father would never do that however hard pressed he was.

'Edmund was always a careful man,' Mr Hampson explained. 'He needed to save to finance his expeditions, but he invested well and wisely. He left ...' He mentioned a fairly large sum. 'There will be estate duty, of course, and as a matter of formality you'll have to prove your identity. You have a birth certificate, passport, marriage certificate, perhaps?'

'My husband has my papers, but not a birth certificate. I can get a copy of that, I suppose?'

'Of course. It was a very sad business about your father, the world has been deprived of a very eminent man. My sympathy, Ann.'

'Thank you. It was a great blow.'

But the knowledge had come to her so gradually that it could hardly be described as a blow, though only now did she realise how completely alone in the world she was except for the Strattons, who did not want her.

Unaware of the true circumstances, Mr Hampson said genially: 'At least you've got a husband to console you. Is he with you? I should like to meet him.'

Angela told him Clive had been unable to get away and her brother-in-law had brought her up to London. Consolation from Clive in that direction had never been forthcoming. It was when she had discovered her loss that he had become remote.

Mr Hampson required her to sign certain documents here and then including a letter of application for her birth certificate, which he said he would obtain for her.

'You're not much like your father,' he observed with the candour of an old family friend, 'the Sullivans were fair. You take more after your mother, perhaps?'

'I don't think I'm much like either of them,' she told him, and remembered Clive had asked her if there was a likeness. It flashed into her mind with a spurt of anger that he must have been wondering if anyone would recognise her as her father's daughter, and merely because his stepmother had an absurd prejudice against her surname.

She took her leave of the old man who had come from behind his professional façade to condole with her. He said he would be communicating with her, and would be glad to help her in any way he could.

She had arranged to meet Ralph for lunch and found the place he had mentioned without difficulty, for London was familiar to her. She wondered how she could counter his questions regarding her morning's activities, but he did not ask any, being too full of his own affairs to notice her abstraction.

His interview had gone well and he was confident that he had landed the job. This, he declared, was his big break, the opportunity for which he had been waiting so long, while Clive's absences tied him to Sherborne.

'Thank heaven he's got himself wed,' he ejaculated jubilantly. 'He won't want to be going off now he's got you around.'

Angela wished she was sure of that.

They went to a matinee of a popular musical, and drove home after the rush hour through the gloaming. Even Ralph's exuberance was a little wilted by fatigue and he relapsed into silence.

As the miles flew by, Angela came to a decision. Whatever maggot had been in Clive's brain when he asked her not to disclose her maiden name, she would no longer obey his wishes. Mrs Stratton could get over her absurd prejudice against her nomenclature, for she would no longer deny her father. Besides, there would be much correspondence coming to her while the estate was being wound up, and it would be a little deceitful to endeavour to conceal what was going on—and why should she? It was time she asserted herself; submissiveness had got her nowhere with Clive and had given his stepmother the idea that she was a nonentity. The discovery that she had means of her own had given her new confidence, and she determined that she would reorganise her life on a more satisfactory basis and have a showdown with Clive. If he wished to be rid of her, she would go, but she would not stand for any more blather about Jasmine.

It was late when they reached Abbotswood and

Angela left the field to Ralph, for it was his day and her own concerns could wait. Celia was not very enthusiastic about his job, her possessive nature shrank from releasing her chick from her maternal apron strings, but Clive congratulated him heartily.

'So I'll have only you left,' Celia said to Clive.

'Don't overlook Angela and no doubt an increasing brood of grandchildren,' Ralph told her lightly.

Mrs Stratton's face darkened.

'Only courtesy grandchildren,' she pointed out acidly. 'Clive isn't really my son. It would have been so different if ...' She sighed pathetically.

If they were Jasmine's, Angela mentally finished the sentence, and caught a sombre look on her husband's face. Had he had the same thought? There would not be any children if he did not change his attitude towards her, but perhaps he did not want them from her. The thought was painful, for Angela would dearly like to have a family.

She had no opportunity to speak to Clive next day, for he left early to go to a stock sale in Devonshire and did not return until very late. She could have gone to him after they retired, but she shrank from doing that, afraid he might think she intended to make another advance, and her pride would not allow her to so cheapen herself.

On the following morning, she received a bulky envelope from Selwyn and Hampson, containing among other documents a copy of her father's will.

They were all seated at the breakfast table, for Mrs Stratton had ceased to take hers upstairs, and since Angela rarely had any mail, they were eyeing the type-written pages curiously.

Ralph said: 'My lord, that all looks very official. Come into a fortune, Angela?'

146

'Sort of,' she returned brightly. 'This is a copy of the last will and testament of my dear father, Edmund Sullivan.'

Dead silence followed her pronouncement. Looking round a little nervously, Angela saw Clive's gaze was fixed apprehensively upon his stepmother, Ralph looked incredulous, while as for Mrs Stratton ...

Celia's face had gone perfectly white and her eyes were glittering, while her hands were tearing savagely at her table napkin; the only sound that filled the quiet room was the noise of rending linen. When at length she spoke, her voice was hoarse:

'Did you say Edmund Sullivan?'

'Yes,' Angela met her glaring eyes bravely. 'He was an archaeologist, you know, and quite famous in his field. I'd been with him on a dig in Persia before he was killed in an air crash ...'

She got no further. Celia had risen from her seat and turned her baleful gaze upon Clive.

'How could you do this to me?'

'Mother ...' he began to expostulate.

'Never call me that again!' her voice rose shrilly. 'You ... you married a girl whose father ruined my daughter ... a thief ... a seducer ...'

White-hot fury welled up in Angela at this libel.

'How dare you slander my father!' she blazed. 'He was as fine and honourable a man who ever walked ...' and then the hideous truth struck her. 'No,' she gasped, 'it wasn't Daddy. It couldn't have been Daddy!'

Celia stared at Angela with intense animosity. 'Fine and honourable indeed! Who are you trying to kid? Wasn't he in Greece in—' She mentioned a date. 'Can you deny that? Oh, I always felt there was something wrong about you under your meek ways, worming yourself in here, but how Clive could ...' she choked.

'He ... he didn't know,' Angela whispered. 'I'd lost my memory.' So this was the reason why Clive had turned from her when he had learned who she was, but his aversion was quite unjustifiable. Her mind went back to that year in Greece, when Edmund had been away a long time. She had missed him badly, for her mother had been more than usually ailing and peevish, and she had been only a schoolgirl. Her mother's continual whine—'He's having a whale of a time, you bet, with all those youngsters on the site, with never a thought for us. Shouldn't be surprised if he never came back at all.'

But Edmund had come back, returning swiftly when he was summoned, for Angela had been very ill, neglected bronchitis turning to pneumonia, and calling weakly for her father. Whatever he felt about his wife, he had loved his child.

The moment's doubt passed like a cold douche as Angela's love and loyalty rose up in revolt against it. The evidence was only circumstantial, and her father could not possibly have stooped to be Jasmine's lover.

She became aware that Clive was making belated explanations to his stepmother and recalled that neither Celia nor Ralph had heard the facts of their meeting before. Briefly he related how Angela had been found and how he had cared for her, not knowing who she was.

Ralph was looking a little stunned, but Celia broke out again into violent vituperation.

'Never heard such a tale! Lost her memory indeed! If she had it was a pretence. She knew very well that if you'd known her identity you'd have pushed her back into that ravine along with her brute of a father.' Her voice changed to passionate appeal. 'Wouldn't you, Clive?' There was almost supplication in her eyes.

'No,' Clive returned. 'She was injured and needed help. Were she fifty times Sullivan's daughter, I'd have tended her.'

'You soft fool!' Celia hissed. She turned her venomous gaze back to Angela. 'To bring you here, to put you in my darling's place—it's enough to bring her out of her grave!'

'Where you've never let her lie,' Ralph interposed. 'Look, Mother, all this happened a decade ago, and even if Edmund Sullivan did have an affair with Jass, which is by no means proved.' Angela threw him a grateful glance. 'Angie's a sweet, nice girl and Clive's darned lucky to get her. So suppose we forget all about what's past and should have been buried long ago.'

Celia looked at her son as if she had never seen him before.

'You too, Ralph,' she said. Froth appeared on her lips and she fell back into her chair, her head on the table. 'Jasmine,' she whispered, and became still.

There was a moment of stunned silence punctuated by Celia's stertorous breathing; Clive threw one reproachful glance at Angela, then bent over his stepmother.

'Ring Doctor Murray, Ralph,' he bade his brother, 'she's had a stroke.'

Ralph ran to the telephone while Clive lifted Mrs Stratton in his arms preparatory to carrying her upstairs, and Angela faltered inadequately: 'I'm sorry, Clive.'

Ignoring her apology, he told her curtly to follow him upstairs. Obediently she crept up the staircase after him and into Celia's room. There, under his instructions, she stripped the bed of its counterpane and pillows so that he could lay his burden down flat. He loosened Celia's clothing and felt for her pulse, his face creased with anxiety. Through the open door to the adjoining dressing room Jasmine gazed down at them in all her luscious beauty. As if suddenly aware of her, Clive jerked up his head and glanced distastefully towards the portrait.

'Please shut that door,' he commanded.

Angela recollected that he disliked that picture of Jasmine, considering it did not do her justice. Noiselessly she slipped across the room and reached for the door handle. The door opened inwards, and involuntarily her eyes turned towards the picture. Jasmine's eyes seemed alive with triumph, for had she not shattered Angela's tranquillity for all time, destroying her cherished image of her father and causing an unbridgeable gulf to open between her and her husband? Angela pulled the door shut and felt a momentary relief when the scornful face was hidden behind it, but the damage was done. Clive would never forgive her for blurting out her identity, but how could she have anticipated the devastating effect of her disclosure, for he had given her no hint of what to expect. Naturally she had never connected her father with Jasmine—the very idea was completely incongruous, and if Clive had ever met Edmund Sullivan, he would know that. She leaned against the closed door watching him with yearning in her eyes. Surely it would have been better if he had told her when she had remembered her name what he believed about her father instead of resorting to the feeble subterfuge of asking her to conceal her surname.

That he did believe the slander and had turned from her as a result was only too painfully obvious. It explained everything that had puzzled her about his behaviour, his withdrawal since that night at Bamian. Only a very genuine feeling for her, in short, love, could overcome his revulsion, and that he had never felt towards her. How bitterly he must regret his refusal to accept her suggestion and wish that he had refrained from making their marriage a reality. Those few nights together had crowned her womanhood and were her most treasured memory, but they had forged a bond between them which now he would be seeking means to break.

Ralph scratched on the outer door and slipped inside. He had caught Doctor Murray before he had set out on his rounds, and he would be with them in a few moments. He looked fearfully at his mother's recumbent form.

'Is there anything I can do?'

Clive shook his head. 'It will be hospital for her, if ...' He broke off, every moment that passed was touch and go with Celia. 'You can take Angela downstairs,' he went on. 'Better give her a drink.'

'I ... I'd rather stay here,' Angela whispered. She wanted to share Clive's vigil, but his eyes were steel as he told her:

'There's nothing you can do here. Go along with Ralph.'

Repulsed, for it was for his sake that she had wanted to stay, she allowed Ralph to lead her out of the room and downstairs, but not into the dining room from whence the maid had not yet cleared the debris of breakfast but into the sitting room. He seemed to bear no rancour for her part in the morning's débâcle. He settled her in an armchair with a cushion behind her back with solicitude, as if she also were an invalid.

'A drop of brandy?' he enquired. 'It'll help you to pull yourself together.'

She refused; she did not need anything, she told him.

'You ought to be hating me,' she added sadly.

'Rubbish,' he said briskly, 'you haven't done anything. Ma's cult of Jass has become a sort of mania with her, and anything can bring on a stroke with people of her age.' He looked at Angela curiously. 'It's life's supreme irony that you and Clive should have been thrown together.'

'Kismet,' she said, and sighed. 'It's the sort of fate that pursues the characters in a Greek drama. In some ways it's quite appropriate,' she laughed drearily. 'There's always been something classical about Clive and his admiration for Greek culture.'

She winced at the memories her words recalled—Clive showing her the Macedonian coin in far-away Nuristan, his interest in the people's supposed Greek origin, and wished she were still the nameless waif of those carefree days, and remembered Clive had wished it also.

The arrival of Doctor Murray cut short further conversation. Ralph took him upstairs and Angela sat on feeling excluded, hearing footsteps going upstairs, the telephone being used, and footsteps reascending. Finally Ralph reappeared.

'An ambulance is coming for her,' he announced. 'Would you go and pack a case for her? Nightwear and so forth—Clive says you'll know better than we should what she'll need.'

Angela went back upstairs thankful to be able to perform some small service. Mrs Stratton's condition was unchanged, and Clive sat beside her holding her hand, as if he hoped by that contact to retain her in life. Ralph brought in a small case and Angela as quietly as possible opened drawers and cupboards extracting nightgowns, slippers, dressing gown and such oddments that she thought the patient might require. She had just finished when the ambulance drew up outside, and throughout her task, Clive had never once looked at her. It struck her as a little strange that he who was not her son was showing much greater concern for Celia than Ralph who was.

That was explained to her later. Celia was taken away, Clive going with her. Ralph was to go to the hospital in the afternoon. Angela went to consult Celia's trainee about food, for even if the heavens were about to fall, men must still eat. She helped the girl, whose name was Maureen, prepared a menu for both lunch and dinner, for she concluded that they would all be present for the latter meal. She was glad to have some occupation and a curious numbness lay over her heart.

Over lunch, Ralph told her:

'Poor old Clive seems to be taking it hard. Ma's always been devoted to him, though she isn't his mother. She absorbed herself in him and Jasmine. Me she hadn't a lot of time for, I was so much younger than they were, and of course,' he grinned wryly, 'I wasn't the heir to Abbotswood. I was sent to boarding school when I was quite small to get me out of the way, and then to college. My old man was all right, but he was getting on and he hadn't a lot to say to a young lad, and he thought a lot more of Clive. It was Clive's mother who was the love of his life, so it's only natural he clung to him. I don't think he'd a lot of time for Jasmine, neither had I. Of course he died before the wedding.'

'Did you go to it?' Angela enquired.

'No. I had measles and was in the school sanatorium, so I missed all the fun,' he told her regretfully. 'Of course I was given a very expurgated account of what happened, but personally I think Clive was well rid of Jasmine.'

'He still grieves for her,' Angela said pensively.

'What after all this while?' Ralph looked astonished. 'Don't you kid yourself, Angel, he's had a whale of a time on those safaris of his, I'm only surprised ...' He stopped and looked embarrassed.

'That he gave up his freedom to marry me,' Angela finished for him. 'But I told him he mustn't feel tied if he wanted to go off again.'

Ralph looked at her oddly. 'What did he say to that?'

'He took me at my word. He was half inclined to join a German expedition to Bolivia until duty brought him home.'

Ralph laughed wholeheartedly. 'I'm not surprised. If my bride on my honeymoon told me she didn't mind if I went to Timbuctoo, I couldn't get away fast enough. Not very flattering, were you, Angel?'

This was such a new point of view that Angela could only stare at him blankly.

'But surely Clive couldn't have imagined that I didn't want him?' she gasped. 'I was being self-sacrificing, or so I thought.'

'Let's hope he appreciated your nobility.'

Angela sighed. 'It doesn't matter whether he did or he didn't now. He'll never forgive me for causing Mrs Stratton to have a stroke, nor for being who I am.'

'Now don't *you* go getting morbid,' Ralph chided her. 'Anything might have caused Ma's stroke, she had a high blood pressure. As for being who you are, you aren't responsible for your pa's sins.'

'No, and I'm perfectly certain he was not responsible for your sister's tragedy.'

'Don't see that it matters much either way—they're both dead.'

'It matters to me. I want to clear his name,' Angela cried vehemently. Except for that one moment of doubt when she had recalled her father's lengthy absence in Greece, she had become more and more convinced that Edmund Sullivan could not have had an intimate connection with Jasmine Stratton. From what she knew of his character and integrity the supposition was simply ludicrous, and it was mere coincidence that his expedition had been in Greece at the same time as she was, an unlucky coincidence since it had caused their names to be linked.

Ralph shrugged his shoulders indifferently.

'Best let sleeping dogs lie,' he advised her. 'You'll only stir up a lot of mud.'

'I intend to vindicate him,' she said stubbornly, though whether by so doing she could change Clive's attitude towards herself she dared hardly hope, it seemed he had gone too far away from her to be recalled, but she could not allow the slur to continue to sully her father's memory.

'My sweet child,' Raph began, 'your loyalty does you credit.' She looked up quickly, dark eyes alert under delicate black brows. Clive had used those very words; he had also said he did not wish to destroy her illusions. That was why he had not told her upon the night when he had related Jasmine's story that he believed her father was the man involved. Her resolution strengthened, for it was Clive, not herself, who was deluded.

'But,' Ralph went on, 'sometimes it's best not to know the truth.'

'Not in this case,' Angela returned firmly. 'I shan't rest until I've discovered it.'

Ralph said he must go to the hospital after lunch, for though he had ascertained over the phone that there was no change, he felt guilty about not sharing Clive's vigil.

'She might regain consciousness and ask for us,' he said jauntily, but Angela was not deceived; he feared that if he were absent too long, she might die while he was not there. She hoped fervently that Mrs Stratton would recover, though her vindictiveness had destroyed the sympathy she would otherwise have felt for her.

Left to herself, she made some phone calls upon her own behalf, for a plan was beginning to evolve, the execution of which depended upon Celia's survival. Clive had been short-sighted, she thought; he should have told her the truth, for he must have known that there was a risk that she might inadvertently betray her identity. Unfortunately she had done it deliberately, being quite unaware of the sinister significance of her disclosure. She hoped desperately that Clive would realise that she had not known what she was doing; he had always treated her with kindness and consideration, but recalling his cold condemnatory eyes when he had last looked at her, she feared that she had trespassed beyond all hope of reconciliation. Where Jasmine and Jasmine's kin were concerned he had neither understanding nor mercy.

She had nothing to do but wait for the two men to return, as presumably they would for dinner. It was one of those occasionally lovely days in May which give a foretaste of the summer to come, but she could not appreciate it. Rain would have been more in keeping with her mood, and the sunshine seemed to mock her.

She dreaded the inevitable encounter with Clive

and the cruel things he might say to her, which would hurt all the more because she so desperately wanted to be able to comfort him.

CHAPTER NINE

WITH a woman's instinct to look her best when confronted by a tricky situation, Angela dressed carefully for dinner. She put on a long cream-coloured gown with a high waist and softly draped bodice. The dress clung to her hips and fell in graceful folds to her feet. It made her look very slender and youthful. The rich black coils of her hair she drew up on to the crown of her head, exposing the slim lines of her long neck, her small ears and wide forehead. A little eye-shadow gave mystery to her big dark eyes, but she used it sparingly, knowing that Clive disliked obvious make-up. She dared not apply any scent, but the lavender sacs which hung among her clothes gave a faint fragrance to her person.

Involuntarily she compared herself with that other dark-haired woman, whose portrait hung in Celia's room. Feature by feature Jasmine had no great advantage, but Angela lacked that sensual exotic aura which emanated from that pictured face. Jasmine epitomised sexual allure, but it seemed to Angela that the simplicity of a naïve schoolgirl still clung to herself. Had she been given to poetic metaphor, she might have described them both as the pure serenity of a lily contrasted with the flamboyance of a crimson peony, but such a flight of fancy would never occur to her.

She went downstairs and surveyed the preparations for the meal. Maureen had stayed later than usual without demur, for she hoped to glean some gossip for distribution at home when her employers returned. She was well aware of drama in the air, but did not know its cause. The mistress had been struck down as if by the hand of God, and according to Maureen's logic, such a visitation did not happen without provocation. That the gentle young Mrs Stratton could have provided it seemed out of character. To Maureen's thinking she was much too meek and mild, and if she had been in Angela's shoes she would have told Mrs Stratton Senior long ago where she belonged, which was not at the head of the dining table or behind the silver tea-pot in Clive's house.

Quite unconscious of her handmaiden's silent championship, Angela expressed her approval and hoped the men would not be late so that Maureen's coq au vin, made under her supervision, would not be spoilt, but at the right time, only Ralph appeared.

'Ma's better,' he announced. 'She's conscious, but she hasn't spoken yet. The doctor thinks she may do so soon.'

'Oh, I'm so glad,' Angela exclaimed with genuine relief. 'But where's Clive?'

'He's staying a little longer. She seems to want him to hold her hand. He'll be along later.'

Angela thought Clive was overdoing the devoted son, for he was not Celia's son, and if she was out of danger he might have come home, but perhaps he felt guilty because the stroke had been caused by his wife's disclosure and was striving to make amends, a thought that made Angela wince. She also suspected that Celia was endeavouring to keep him from her and using her

158

helplessness to chain him to her bedside. Even in her extremity her possessiveness was paramount.

Meanwhile Ralph was appraising her elegant appearance.

'Dolled up, aren't you, love?' he said appreciatively. 'Does me good to see something truly feminine after all those starched uniforms, but I don't flatter myself you've done it for my benefit.'

'Oh, I like to make myself look nice in the evening,' Angela told him, hoping Clive would be similarly impressed. A doubt struck her. 'But perhaps I shouldn't have changed. Does it seem heartless?'

'Oh, for the lord's sake—we aren't in mourning yet,' Ralph exclaimed.

'Well, if Clive isn't coming, we'd better go and eat,' Angela suggested, only half reassured.

Ralph did justice to the coq au vin, but Angela merely picked at her portion for the ordeal of meeting Clive still hung over her. She arranged with Maureen to put something to keep warm for him in the cool oven, one of the features of the Aga stove. Then Ralph announced that he was going for a ride.

'Want to get the smell of disinfectant out of my nose,' he explained. 'Why don't you come along? Blow the cobwebs away.'

She declined this invitation, for to ride she would have to change and she wanted to be there when Clive arrived.

'I wouldn't like him to come back to an empty house,' she explained.

'He'll be in a filthy mood,' Ralph warned her.

Angela's heart sank. Ralph was telling her what to expect. For a moment she wavered. It would be pleasant to get out and away on this beautiful sunlit evening and postpone the inevitable showdown, but it would only be postponing it, better to get it over and done with.

'He's had a trying day,' she pointed out to excuse her husband.

'And you as a good little wife are hoping to provide soothing syrup,' Ralph jibed. 'I wish you luck, my Angel.'

He went off whistling to change before going to the stables. His mother's illness did not seem to weigh upon his spirits, but always an optimist, he was already convinced of her complete recovery, and he too had had a trying day.

Angela stood at the window to watch him ride away, a gay and gallant figure in boots, breeches and sweater on a skittish chestnut horse. Disdaining a hat, the speed of his going blew his black hair in disorder about his brown face, giving him a rakish air. Actually he was more her contemporary than Clive, but she felt definitely elder-sisterly towards him; she wished Clive had more of his half-brother's sanguine temperament, but then he would not be Clive, whose faults as much as his virtues constituted the make-up of the man she loved.

Feeling restless and apprehensive, she strolled out into the garden, after putting a fleecy stole over her shoulders, for though it had been a warm day it still turned chilly at night. The lovely evening light lay over the profusion of spring blossoms and flowering trees, which made May the most beautiful of all the months. The first of the roses were in bud showing colour, and a trellis covered with honeysuckle filled the air with fragrance. For Angela it had been a long spring, starting with the melting of the snows in Nuristan, which seemed an aeon ago, followed by her marriage and the ill-starred expedition to Bamian. It was a long way from the colossal figure of Buddha to this English garden and it seemed impossible it could only have been a few weeks since she had stared at its scarred face and her memory had returned to her.

The calm beauty all around her soothed her taut nerves. She crossed the lawn and went down the steps through the rockery into the rose garden beyond. A bat flitted across the rose and amber sky, somewhere in the trees an owl hooted. Angela sat down on a rustic bench, and it was there that Clive found her when at last he returned. She looked enticing enough to disarm any irate husband the soft folds of her dress falling about her, the stole slipping from her shoulders to display arms, neck, and delicate profile, old ivory in the last of the daylight against the dark background of the shrubbery.

But Clive was in no mood to be enticed. He came striding down from the lawn above with obvious purpose. He still wore the slacks and pullover of breakfast time, having had no opportunity to change, and his face was pale and drawn with lines of weariness and anxiety, his mouth set in a grim line.

Angela, glancing nervously towards him as he approached, saw that his eyes were very cold. Grey eyes, she thought with a shiver, could appear glacial.

She stood up and asked timidly: 'Would you like your dinner, Clive, it's being kept warm for you.'

'Later.' He dismissed food with a wave of his hand.

'Ralph says Mrs Stratton is better,' Angela went on. 'I'm so glad.'

'She'll live,' he told her succinctly, 'but no thanks to you.' His expression became accusatory. 'Didn't I tell you not to mention the name of Sullivan in her presence?'

'You did, but you didn't tell me why,' she said reproachfully. 'You should have done, for it was bound to come out sooner or later, and I don't like evasion and pretence. I'd no idea what you all believed about my father, which I'm sure isn't true, until it all came out at breakfast. I too had a shock, Clive.'

Her dark eyes were full of appeal, but his did not soften.

'Not half the shock it gave me at Bamian when I discovered I'd married Edmund Sullivan's daughter,' he returned. 'Of all the women in the world you're the one who out of common decency I should have avoided.'

He was as prejudiced as his stepmother, and Angela's drooping spirits flared up at the injustice of his pronouncement.

'Why?' she demanded fiercely. 'Has the libel you've fastened upon my father made me into a pariah? Is that what's come between us? You're being unreasonable, Clive.'

'I don't think so. I've been very forbearing.'

'By keeping away from me? I'm to be perpetually deprived of my husband because I happen to have been born a Sullivan.'

'No, not because of that,' he said to her surprise. 'I asked you to be patient, you'll remember.'

'I see no need for patience,' she returned stormily. 'Nor can there be any other reason for your withdrawal. I'd appreciate more candour from you, Clive, instead of these continual evasions. If you'd told me on that night when I ... when I came to you what you had against me instead of rambling on about the sorrows of Jasmine, what happened this morning would have been avoided.'

'I couldn't,' he said so gently, that she was astonished. 'You were so certain of your father's integrity, it would have been cruel to enlighten you.'

'And are you so certain you're not mistaken?' she demanded.

'I am.'

His confident tone roused her ire. He permitted no shadow of doubt, and with her whole soul she rejected the aspersion cast upon her father's honour.

'Then let me tell you, you're quite wrong,' she cried, her voice quivering. 'Daddy couldn't have had an affair with Jasmine.'

'You were only a child, it would be easy to deceive you,' he told her, adding with pitying contempt: 'Poor Angela!'

He turned aside and picked a white rosebud, staring at its unfolding petals absently.

'I don't want your pity,' she fumed. 'That's all you've ever given me, isn't it? Pity!'

He seemed about to speak, checked himself and returned to his contemplation of the rosebud. Angela gazed yearningly at his bent head, half averted from her. She wanted to put her arms around him, beg him to let her comfort and soothe him, for was it not her place to do so? She was still his wife, and once he had desired her. She made a movement towards her and as if sensing her purpose, he drew back—only a yard at most, but it showed her how completely he was alienated from her.

'What happens now?' she asked drearily. 'I suppose you'll never forgive me for what happened this morning.'

'I hope I'm not so vindictive,' he said with a touch of hauteur. He paused, glanced at her and then went on almost apologetically: 'I'm very fond of Celia, Angela, and I owe her a lot. I'd lost my own mother, remember, and she made no difference between me and her own child. I hate to see her hurt. She's had a lot of sorrow, she's lost two husbands as well as her adored daughter.'

'I appreciate all that, but it's no reason why she should be so beastly to me,' Angela told him with more warmth than wisdom.

Clive threw her a quick steely glance.

'I hadn't noticed she was being beastly to you. It seemed to me that she made you very welcome.'

The blind obtuseness of the male—Celia's innuendoes and deliberate malice had passed him by. Angela choked back angry words. How could he have failed to notice that she had been continually humiliated by comparisons with Jasmine to her disadvantage? But perhaps he had been making the same comparisons himself and found her lacking. The thought was painful, though by no means a new one. Gathering dignity around her with her stole, she drew herself up and said frigidly:

'Since you so obviously prefer your stepmother to me, there's no need to continue with this farce of a marriage any longer.'

He stared at her in astonishment, his fingers worrying the frail flower he held.

'What on earth do you mean by that?'

'That I'm tired of being treated like a cypher. I've no place here at Abbotswood, where I'm only an unwanted guest.'

'You can take over the reins at any time,' he pointed out, 'Mother was only deputising for you until you'd found your feet.'

But that was not Angela's real grievance. With Celia ill, she would be expected to run the house in any case, but to be merely Clive's housekeeper was no solace for being banished from his arms. Wanting to pierce his indifference, drive him into some show of feeling, she announced acidly:

'You'd find me inadequate, I'm sure, and now I've means of my own I need impose no longer upon your generosity and your pity. I only accepted them because I had no option.'

He dropped the maltreated rosebud and came towards her, his hands clamping down upon her shoulders like a vice.

'You're saying you only married me because you were destitute?' His voice was dangerously quiet, but the glint in his eyes betrayed that she had reached him at last.

'I wouldn't be the first woman to marry for a meal ticket,' she told him.

'I'd never have believed you could be so mercenary.' He stared down into her defiant dark eyes. 'I thought you were still half a child, a sweet submissive creature without guile, whose naïve simplicity had not yet been corrupted.'

This description galled her—he was making her sound like a credulous teenager all goo-eyed for his favours, and at the back of her mind was the image of Jasmine, the epitome of sophisticated allurement.

'It's always easy to deceive a man, particularly when one wants something,' she said airily.

'Is that so?' he enquired slowly. 'So you took me for a sucker. I remember now you suggested a marriage without consummation. Were you trying to evade full payment?' She made a small sound of dissent, but he went on without heeding her: 'You also were complacent about any future expeditions which would take me far away from you. You were insistent I shouldn't consider myself tied. All very charming, and it only occurs to me now that that was an unnatural attitude for a new bride to take.'

Just what Ralph had implied, but how could Clive so misunderstand her? At the time he had seemed pleased by her compliance, but now he was deliberating misinterpreting her motives.

'You've got it all wrong,' she said breathlessly, for his fingers were digging relentlessly into her shoulder and though his touch was so ungentle tremors were running down her spine, but not for worlds would she betray how he was affecting her. 'It was because I wanted you...'

'Sounded like it, didn't it?' he interrupted. 'You didn't want me, Angela, you've just admitted that you were only after what I could give you.'

'So what?' she asked angrily. She had been about to say that she had wanted him because she loved him, but his stupidity enraged her. Didn't he know? Couldn't he see? Apparently not, for he went on bitterly, having accepted her rash words as the truth:

'Like the rest of your sex your innocent airs conceal the little go-getter you really are. Now you've come into money you're proposing to leave me, since I've served my turn. Isn't that what you said?' as she again tried to interrupt. 'But it's a pity that you couldn't have controlled that indiscreet tongue of yours before you departed. Now you're leaving havoc behind you, but perhaps you'd have created worse havoc if you'd stayed, so maybe Abbotswood will be well rid of you, and we can have some peace.'

She had made no allowance for the fact that he was tired and overstrained after a long day of anxiety at the hospital, and since she was responsible for the crisis he was in no mood to be conciliatory. She could have reminded him that when she had sought him on that memorable night he had repelled her with a vague promise that the situation would right itself in time, an attempt to stall her. He had never professed to return the love he seemed to expect from her and ever since he had learned her identity he had withdrawn from her. He was far more to blame than she was for their estrangement, and now he was twisting all her words to show her in a reprehensible light.

She would have been wiser to say no more until he was in a better mood, but her own pain and resentment were welling up in a wild desire to hit back. Searching for words to hurt, she said scornfully:

'Perhaps you believe that wives like children should only speak when they're spoken to. You've always expressed contempt for women. You condescended to marry me only because you thought I was a poor little waif who would be utterly subservient to you, for you're a despot at heart, Clive. You'd like me to approach you on bended knee, wouldn't you, and address you as "Presence" like you said the Afghan women do. You're only sorry you can't shut me up in purdah, which is where you said all women should be kept.'

'You're talking rubbish,' he said through his teeth.

'I'm only quoting your own words back to you,' she said sweetly, and he reddened uncomfortably. Pleased with this sign of discomfort, she went on recklessly:

'You're furious with me because I dared to assert myself. Is it a sin to want to acknowledge one's parentage?'

'You chose the wrong time and company.' He lifted his head arrogantly. 'I suppose it's too much to expect you to respect your husband's wishes, much less obey him.'

'I'm not a harem slave,' she flashed. 'You've no right to insist that I conceal my name as if it were something to be ashamed of.' She saw him frown, and rushed on: 'I forgot you think it is, but I'm not with you there. Take your hands off me, you're hurting me! If this is how you treated Jasmine I'm not surprised that she bolted!'

He almost threw her away from him.

'For God's sake leave her out of it!'

'How can I, when I'm confronted by her at every turn? You can't forget her, can you, Clive? You're as obsessed by her as your stepmother is.'

'Shut up!' he bade her curtly.

'I won't shut up!' All the doubts and fears she had been suffering since coming to England boiled up and overflowed. 'Nor will I stay here and share you with her. Now I'm independent I can snap my fingers at you, your stepmother and Jasmine too ... Clive!'

She cried his name in an onrush of fright and apprehension, for he had swept her up into a merciless hold, and his face was contorted with fury. She had never seen him really lose his temper before and the violence of his rage appalled her.

'Snap your fingers, will you, my girl?' he snarled. 'I'll teach you who's master here and where your loyalty belongs. Kindness and forbearance are useless with women. This ... and this ... is all they want and understand!'

There was no love or tenderness in his punishing kisses. Angela lay helpless in his arms, well aware that, his control having snapped, he was motivated only by a desire to subdue and dominate her, to show her that though she might have tried to flout him, in the end she was powerless before his masculine strength. He turned towards the shrubbery, and guessing his intent, she whispered urgently:

'No, not here, not now ... someone might come ...'

'Who cares? This is my ground, you're my wife,' he muttered thickly.

He was in the grip of primitive desire, seeking release from the tensions of the day in the solace of his woman.

Angela's reluctance melted away. She had longed for her husband's embraces and now he was about to take her again. Her body went limp and excitement set her pulses hammering. The golden glow had vanished from the sky submerged in the purple haze of the falling dusk, for the sun had gone down. The fragrance of flowers scented the still air, and from their treetop the doves were softly calling, mate to mate. Angela's hair, which was never too secure, fell from its bonds to drape them both, as Clive pushed his way into the bushes. A bramble caught at her bare arm, drawing blood as their passage wrenched it away. She did not feel it. Her whole being was submerged in his.

From the lawn above them Maureen called:

'Mr Stratton! Mr Stratton! Doctor Murray's on the phone.'

He stopped and his arms went slack. Angela could feel the apprehension in him. He dropped her unceremoniously among the rosemary, laurel, and other bushes, so abruptly that she nearly fell.

'I'm coming!'

He left her then, leaping up the steps through the rockery, and running across the lawn, his passion doused by the chill of fear. The aromatic scent of rosemary was sharp in Angela's nostrils, as she made her way out of the shrubbery, her pretty dress smeared, its bodice torn by Clive's impatient fingers. Rosemary for remembrance; Celia was inevitably connected with Jasmine in Clive's mind and Jasmine had again defeated her supplanter. Angela stood in the rose garden, twisting up her hair, feeling lonely and desolate. She picked up her stole which had fallen when Clive had lifted her and put it about her shoulders, aware that she was very cold. She hoped desperately the doctor had not rung up to say Celia was sinking for Clive would consider she was little short of a murderess if she died. At her feet, gleaming palely in the dusk was the rosebud Clive had thrown away. Hating to see a flower discarded, she raised it in her fingers, but it was too crushed and broken to be resuscitated. She dropped it, thinking it was symbolic of the way he had trampled on her heart. Idly he had plucked the bud to give him a moment's pleasure and had cast it aside when it had ceased to interest him.

Wearily she went back towards the house, dreading to hear the news that might await her there.

Mrs Stratton, however, was better, and Doctor Murray, an old family friend, had made a late night call at the hospital and had rung Clive to tell him that she had spoken his name and was now sleeping naturally.

Ralph came in while Clive was eating a belated meal, to arrange their plans for the following day. Angela sat at a little distance from them, huddled in her stole. She had brought Clive's food in to him and he had thanked her perfunctorily, avoiding her eyes. She sensed that he was ashamed of his violence in the garden, but was too incensed against her to apologise. Ralph glanced at her from time to time, noticing with concern her pale face and shadowed eyes. He brought her a glass of wine and insisted that she drank it. Angela caught Clive's sardonic smile and wondered if he thought she was trying to subjugate his half-brother now.

Ralph said kindly: 'Better go to bed, Angel, you look worn out.'

'I think I will.' She stood up and looked appealingly at Clive, but he turned his head away.

'Goodnight,' he said gruffly. So she was not to be forgiven. She had half hoped he would come up with her to complete what had been interrupted in the garden, but it was obvious all passion was dead in him now, and he had reverted to his previous mood of censure. Wearily she climbed the stairs and went into her own room. Her relations with her husband seemed to be hopelessly wrecked and her best course was to go away and start a new life, but before she closed this chapter of her stormy existence, there was still a task she had to perform. Whether if she carried it out successfully it would make any difference she did not know, but she was determined to try. She must vindicate her father.

Angela decided to go up to London next day. She did not see Clive, he had gone out early, but Ralph was there, and after giving her instructions to Maureen who seemed quite pleased to be left in charge, she told him she had business to attend to and would spend the night at a hotel.

'In connection with your inheritance, I suppose?' He looked at her awkwardly. 'Don't take all this too much to heart. Mother's never been quite sane about Jassy, and she's going to recover.'

'Clive will never forgive me.'

'Of course he will, it wasn't your fault. How could you have known your name was like a red rag to a bull? Besides, she isn't his mother, and if I can exonerate you, he must.' As Angela still looked doubtful, he smiled and patted her shoulder. 'I daresay it's not a bad idea to go away for a few days. Give him time to get his priorities right.'

Of which I'm not one, she thought, and said aloud:

'Just what occurred to me.'

'I'll miss you, Angel, so don't stop away too long.'

Balm to her sore heart. Why could not Clive be as magnanimous? But Clive had been married to Jasmine, and Ralph, from what he had said, had not liked his half-sister, so he would feel no resentment against her lover, and her lover's daughter, but Angela was out to prove that Edmund Sullivan had never been that.

Angela went to see Mr Hampson. Could he, she enquired, give her any information about Edmund Sullivan's expedition to Greece in 19..? Did he know anyone who had accompanied her father, who could tell her the names of the personnel engaged, for she wanted to discover if Jasmine Stratton had been among their number. Mr Hampson was perplexed and a little suspicious. It was a long time ago and he could remember no details, but if she really needed some information she could look up Jack Forest.

'He was a very old friend of your father's, and I believe he sponsored that dig. He went with them and could tell you anything you want to know. I'll get my secretary to ring and find out if he's in town. He lives in Hampstead.'

Jack Forest was, and was surprised and delighted to learn that Angela had survived the air crash. He would welcome a visit from her at any time. Angela taxied out to Hampstead that same afternoon in a mood of mingled triumph and trepidation. If anyone could tell her the truth it would be this Mr Forest, but would he? If Edmund Sullivan had been having an affair would he disclose it to his daughter, or was it not more likely he would try to cover up for him? Somehow she must convince him that the knowledge was essential to her, and at least he would confirm whether or not Jasmine had been on that expedition.

There was no doubt about Jack Forest's passion for antiquity. Every article in his house breathed history, from the ancient armour in the hall, swords, duelling pistols and cutlasses adorning its walls, to the Greek and Egyptian ornaments in his sitting room. Angela had met him several times during her schooldays and had thought he looked like a mummy himself, with his brown wizened face redeemed from ugliness by the intelligent dark eyes. He had never married. The appearance of the room into which she was shown by his houseman was a little startling. There was a mummy case in one corner with a gilded mask, and a statue of a nymph in another. There were cases of statuettes of the sort found in Egyptian tombs and Greek vases on carved tables. But the chairs and settee were Victorian, except for several wooden ones which she thought must be Sheraton. Mr Forest did not seem to mind mixing his periods; the only consistency about the room was that nothing was modern. Even the curtains looked like tapestry and the floor covering was a Persian carpet. Glancing at the undoubtedly valuable antiques, Angela rememberd Clive's indictment. Some of the articles might have been smuggled into the country, for their counterparts were only to be found in museums. A large white cat was ensconced in the best chair, which gave her one disdainful glance, then went back to sleep again.

She had waited some time, and when Jack Forest did appear, he had obviously not spent the time tidying himself. His old velvet jacket was dusty with cigarette ash, his trousers were baggy, and he wore a little black skull cap on his mane of untidy silvery hair. He begged her to excuse his appearance; he had not expected her to arrive so soon.

'I was in the middle of unpacking a case of ancient papyrus that has been sent to me to decipher. I am, you know, an expert on hieroglyphics. They are of absorbing interest and I forgot the time.'

Angela apologised for disturbing him.

'Not at all, my dear,' he said kindly. 'I'm honoured that a young and attractive woman can spare a moment to visit an old fogey like me. You must have some tea.' He pressed a bell. 'I was shocked to hear of poor Eddy's death, when was it, six ... eight months ago ... but rejoiced that you escaped. You've grown into a very beautiful woman, Ann—you remind me of the head of Queen Nefertiti. You know it, of course? And so smart,' he went on, eyeing her becoming two-piece. 'Amazing how time flies, it seems only yesterday that you wore a ponytail and a gym-slip. Oh, I was so delighted when Hampson told me you were alive. It's so sad when young lives are cut short.'

Tea was brought in to them by the houseman, a Japanese, in a Queen Anne silver tea-pot. There were cucumber sandwiches and a rich plum cake.

'I hope it's to your liking, ma'am,' he said. 'The master never notices what he eats.'

Angela assured him that it all looked delicious.

It was some time before she could bring her host to the subject about which she had come to enquire. She told him about her marriage, and watched eagerly to see if the name Stratton rang a bell, apparently it did not. Finally she mentioned the expedition to Greece and the date.

'Ah yes, we were in search of Argive tombs. They think they've found the graves of Agamemnon and Menelaus, but they're not verified. For a long time they were thought to be mythical characters, but then so was Troy until Schliemann discovered it by follow-

174

ing the directions in the Iliad. There's still a vast amount of research to be done on those sites.'

'I'm sure there is.' She couldn't care less. 'Mr Forest,' she said earnestly, 'this is important to me. Can you recollect who went on that trip with you? Were there any women?'

'To be sure there were, though I don't consider it's women's work. They don't make good archaeologists, because women are rarely dedicated to one subject and when they go on digs, too often they have an ulterior motive, and we had an unfortunate example of that on that expedition.'

'Yes?' Angela prompted breathlessly as he paused. 'Do you remember who she was?'

'I haven't had much to do with women, but I knew that one was a wrong 'un the moment she entered the aircraft. She'd got poor old Eddy twisted round her little finger.' Angela's heart sank at this pronouncement. 'It appeared that she had attended a course of lectures he gave on Greece during the winter which she declared had roused in her an intense interest in Grecian monuments, also she had contributed handsomely towards our funds, so I suppose he felt bound to take her. Caused trouble right from the start by turning up at the last moment. Eddy thought she wasn't coming and hadn't made a reservation for her. I don't remember many of the others, but I couldn't forget her. Wild tempestuous sort of creature and about as genuinely interested in digging as that cat. Beautiful, isn't she? The cat, I mean, the only female I've ever lived with,' he chuckled at what he considered a risqué joke. 'Sleeps on my bed at night.'

'This girl,' Angela recalled him to the point. 'Do you remember her name?'

He wrinkled his brow. 'Lawson, I think it was,' and

Angela felt relieved, until she recalled that Jasmine's maiden name would not be Stratton and she had never heard it mentioned. Nor were Jack Forest's next words reassuring. 'Of course it was old Eddy she was after,' he told her. 'Your father was a good-looking fellow, my dear, but he didn't realise what she was up to—however, that didn't stop her from playing the field. She created havoc among the team and what was worse, she became involved with our Greek helpers. A big expedition employs a lot of native labour, as I expect you know, to do the heavy work and some of those Greeks were very handsome. Greeks are passionate and jealous, and when they started knifing each other over her favours, Eddy said she must go home.' He paused and looked at Angela doubtfully. 'It isn't a very pretty story for a young lady to hear.'

'Tell me one thing, can you remember the girl's Christian name?'

He looked perplexed. 'I know it was something outlandish. I've no use for fancy names myself. My mother was called Mary, and you're Ann...'

'Yes,' she was torturing the strap of her handbag in her suspense, 'sensible names, I'm sure ... Was hers Jasmine?'

He looked blank and then suddenly his face cleared.

'Jassy, that's what they called her. I remember now because I thought at first it was Jessie. Brassy would have been more appropriate.'

'Please, Mr. Forest, tell me everything,' Angela besought him. 'I ... I know this girl's relatives and they're slandering my father, so I've come to you to learn the truth.'

'What, after all this while? But if they're anything like her I'm not surprised. Venomous, she was. Well, Eddy had her on the carpet and he asked me to be present in the tent, he'd that much sense, and a good thing I was there too. She wept and raved, declaring that she adored him, she'd only come because of him, she'd left her husband because of him ... the first we'd heard of a husband, by the way ... but he was so cold, so unresponsive, she'd been forced to console herself with others who appreciated her more.'

'Perhaps she really did care for him,' Angela said doubtfully, feeling a sudden sympathy for Jasmine; she too knew the pain of love unrequited.

'Not her. His attraction for her was his indifference. If he'd had the bad taste to flirt with her she'd soon have tired of him. But you know your father, he was dedicated to his work, and to dally with a woman when he was on a dig would have seemed sacrilege to him. I don't think he ever looked at a woman other than your mother.'

'I'm sure he didn't,' Angela exclaimed, delighted to have her faith confirmed, 'but what happened then?

'He got rid of her in the end by telling her if she was married and her passport showed her as single, he'd report her to the authorities, who might put her in prison. She went home next day vowing she'd kill herself, and that was that.'

Falteringly Angela told him of Jasmine's end and the suspicion attached to it.

'Well, it wasn't on Eddy's account,' Mr Forest said emphatically. 'More like it was the Greek boy Nikomedes she misbehaved with. She tried to get him to marry her before she left, but Greek men don't marry ... ahem, naughty girls; besides, by her own admission she wasn't free.' The light of battle came into the bright eyes which were so young in his old face. 'If anyone's casting aspersions on Eddy's character, you refer 'em to me, my girl. I'll soon scotch 'em!'

'Mission accomplished,' Angela said aloud when she finally managed to extract herself from Jack Forest and was on her way back to her hotel.

Her faith in her father had been justified and she could tell Clive that he had been under a misapprehension all these years, and he had no cause to regret having married Edmund Sullivan's daughter; but beyond the satisfaction of being proved right, where would that get her? Clive did not love her; if he did, it would not have mattered to him what her father had done. He was still obsessed by Jasmine's memory, so that it would be cruel to tell him all she had learned that afternoon, from which it was only too obvious Jasmine had been a thoroughly bad lot. It was one thing for Clive to believe she had left him because she could not resist a grand passion for a man who had enticed her away from him, quite another to discover that she had, as Mr Forest put it, played the field. Now that her husband blamed her for causing his stepmother's stroke, she was irretrievably alienated from him, so that it seemed her only course was to leave him, and she would leave him with his illusions intact. He had refused to destroy hers when he had thought she was deluded about her father, and she could equal him in generosity.

But hadn't she already left him when she booked her room at the hotel? Hadn't she known then that she would never go back? She had no place in that stricken household where Jasmine reigned supreme. Only Ralph had any regard for her, and he would be coming to London soon. Clive's real wife, his mate, was the ghost of the girl he had never ceased to regret.

She would write to him and tell him of her decision, which would not be wholly unexpected after that scene in the garden. How easily he had been convinced that she had only married him out of expediency, he could not believe anything good of a Sullivan. She would not undeceive him about that either, since he did not want her love. Everything he had done had been motivated by Jasmine; his exile in Nuristan was due to her, even the consummation of their marriage had been influenced by her. She had cheated him, he had said, so he meant to have fulfilment from his second wife. Had he ever done anything that did not have its root in his passion for Jasmine?

Recalling the beautiful, wilful face Angela realised how foolish she had been to ever dream she could fight her influence. The marvel was that Edmund Stratton had been able to resist her, but thank God he had.

Angela went to bed and since her mind was made up, slept soundly, only to have her decision revoked next morning. For she was horribly sick, and wondering what she could have eaten to upset her so much a sudden suspicion shot into her mind and she began to calculate dates.

She would have to go back to Abbotswood, for it was possible that she was going to bear Clive's child.

CHAPTER TEN

ANGELA lingered in London for another few days. She wanted to make certain that her suspicion was correct, and that entailed a visit to a doctor and a laboratory test. The doctor she went to was the one who had attended her family, so she was no stranger to him, and he too had heard she had perished with her father and was surprised and delighted to find that she had survived, and had a husband to take care of her.

'I brought you into the world, Ann,' he told her, 'though you'll hardly remember that.'

'I hope you'll attend me too.'

'Past it now, I'm afraid. I'm retiring soon and I'm not up in all the latest obstetrics—besides,' he glanced at his notes, 'you live in the country.'

'I could come up for consultations.'

'Better to stay quiet at home. Doubtless your husband has his own doctor whom he would prefer to look after you.'

That brought her back to Clive and the question of his reaction to her news. Would he be pleased—or dismayed? But now there was going to be a living bond between them he would have to become reconciled to her.

She telephoned Abbotswood to give the time of her arrival and ask for a car to meet her at the station. It was Ralph who answered her call.

'Thank goodness you're coming back!' he exclaimed. 'The house has been dead without you and it's several weeks until I take up my new job.'

He had had to give a month's notice.

'How is Mrs Stratton?' she asked anxiously.

'Improving, but I'll give you all the news when I come to meet you.'

She hung up thinking how much she would miss him when he left Abbotswood; he had done so much to make her stay there endurable.

But it wasn't Ralph who was waiting on the platform for her train to arrive.

Her heart leapt as she caught sight of him. Although casually dressed he stood out among the nondescript collection of people waiting for the train, his bared head proudly held, very much the lord of the Manor. He saw her at once and came striding towards her to take her case.

'So you've come back,' he observed. Impossible to decide from his inscrutable expression whether he was pleased or otherwise.

'Didn't you expect me to?'

He gave her a sidelong look as they walked out of the station.

'I was beginning to think you'd run out on me.' He laid his hand upon her arm to steer her towards his car.

'I did think of it,' she admitted.

He smiled wryly. 'I don't seem very successful in keeping wives, but I should have come after you, you know.'

'Would you, Clive?' she asked eagerly.

He unlocked the car and put her case on the back seat, then stepped aside to let her get in. Standing in the open doorway, he looked down at her enigmatically.

'Yes, to ask your pardon. I said some rotten things to you that evening and I lost control of myself. The last thing I wanted ...' he broke off and smiled ruefully. 'You must admit you were provocative—still, I should have known better. Not surprising you rushed off to London, but if we are to part, I couldn't let it be in anger.'

He closed the door and walked round the car to get into his seat, while Angela felt dashed. She had hoped he was going to say he could not do without her, but he seemed to have accepted the possibility of separation, perhaps even welcomed it.

He slid in beside her and drove away in silence; they

soon left the main road and Angela thought how quiet and restful the country seemed after the roar of London traffic. They were wending their way along the green valley bottom. A flight of pigeons circled overhead, disturbed by their passage; hayfields drowsed in the afternoon warmth unaware of approaching decapitation. It was pastoral England at its best.

Rousing herself from her depressing thoughts, she enquired politely after his stepmother and he confirmed that she was improving.

'She won't be coming back to Abbotswood,' he told her. 'She'll need careful nursing for some time and after that I shall make other arrangements.'

Information which came as a great relief to Angela.

'Can we stop?' she asked, resolving she could wait no longer to advise him of his fatherhood. 'I've something to tell you.'

He obligingly drew on to the verge and killed the engine.

'I think I know what it is,' he told her, and she glanced at him in surprise, for surely he could not have guessed, but it seemed his thoughts were running on totally different lines, for he went on: 'And I've something to say to you. I'm thinking of selling Abbotswood.'

'Oh no!' she exclaimed involuntarily.

'The place is a great tie, and expensive to run,' he explained. 'It isn't as if Ralph cared about it. Once he's settled in the swinging city, we shan't see much of him. When I'm free of it, I can be off to the ends of the earth if I'm so inclined.'

He was gazing through the windscreen as if he already saw distant mountains and desert.

Angela's heart sank. So he was itching to be off on his travels again. Even Abbotswood could not hold him, much less herself. He would not be pleased to learn about the child.

'You're taking it for granted that I'm leaving,' she said tartly, concealing her hurt.

'Aren't you? Isn't that what you wanted to tell me? Now you're comfortably off there's nothing to keep you here. I'll be glad for you to stay until you get your money. It'll take some time to sell the place.'

'Big of you to offer me shelter,' she scoffed. 'But do you really want to wander? Don't you want a home?'

'It seems I'm not destined to have one,' he said heavily. 'Bricks and mortar don't constitute a home, Angela. Of course it would be different if I had a son.' He sighed.

This remark was definitely more hopeful. She turned in her seat to look at him directly.

'We could have one,' she murmured shyly, but he kept his profile towards her, shaking his head.

'You'd do better to find a younger man,' he said gently. 'I've watched you with Ralph—youth turns to youth. What happened to the young man who let you down? Perhaps he'll change his mind now you're wealthy.' His lip curled cynically.

'He married someone else,' she told him flatly. 'And I wouldn't have him at any price.' There was no comparison between Arthur and Clive.

'There are other fish in the sea...'

'Oh, for crying out loud!' she exclaimed in exasperation. 'I'm married to you, Clive——' He threw her an odd glance. 'Surely it can't be you're so bigoted as to shrink from Daddy's grandchildren?'

He turned his head and stared at her blankly. 'What an absurd idea! You're not your father, your family is quite immaterial.'

'Since when did you come to that conclusion?' she

asked surprised.

'To tell the truth I *was* completely thrown when you said you were Ann Sullivan. Your name was anathema in our house and I didn't see how I could take you to Abbotswood. There seemed only one way out, to vanish into the Bolivian jungle and leave the way clear for you to divorce me, but I had to come home and I couldn't abandon you. Then I began to think more rationally, and I was sure once Mother got to know you she would be reconciled.'

'Unfortunately she wasn't, and some time, but not now, I'll prove to you how mistaken you've all been about poor Daddy.' She saw disbelief in his face. 'Oh yes, I can do it. I've been to see a certain Mr Jack Forest—you've heard of him?'

'Another of your precious archaeologists. Yes, I've heard of him.'

'He went on that expedition, and he gave me the true facts.'

'So that's what you've been doing up in town, digging up a past which is better buried. I must say you're a loyal daughter, whatever else you are, but I'm not particularly interested.'

'Then you ought to be. I didn't like the nasty aspersions being thrown at him, he was one of the best of men ...' Angela began heatedly.

Clive held up his hand to stop her:

'Okay, okay, I'll believe you.' His face was sombre and it flashed into her mind that he must suspect that to exonerate Edmund she would have to blacken Jasmine and he did not want to know the truth.

'Then why, if the past is immaterial, did you change towards me, Clive? I thought it must be your antagonism towards Daddy, or you found you couldn't forget Jasmine.'

184

He grinned wickedly. 'Well, of course, forbidden fruit is always attractive, and I was hard put to it to keep away from you, but the truth is ...' he hesitated, 'I didn't want to get you pregnant.'

Angela's new-found confidence withered like frail blossoms before a frost. So he did not want children, he did not wish for them because they might preclude his expeditions. Though he had given up the Bolivian scheme he had other projects in mind when Abbotswood's affairs were settled and the place was sold. What was she to do? Tell him his caution had come too late? That the first rapturous days of their union had borne fruit? Or should she conceal the knowledge from him, let him go wherever he wished to go and bear her child in solitude? She had not known until that moment how much she had counted upon her news to effect a reconciliation. She turned away from him to look out of the window to hide her quivering lips, and the peaceful scene was blurred before her eyes. It was some moments before she became aware of what he was saying:

'... so much to do straightening out poor Mother's blunders, and I knew I must keep it from her. Once she suspected she'd have made the hell of a scandal in the hope of driving you away, because I'm afraid she did resent you ...'

'Clive, what are you talking about?'

'Please don't be upset, darling, but when I consulted a solicitor in Sherborne, he told me he didn't think our marriage in Kabul was valid in England, and I should get it put right as soon as possible, but I rather shrank from telling you we'd have to have another wedding, and there was poor Mother to circumvent. It seemed best to have a register office ceremony in London which she wouldn't know about, but that meant one of us had to be domiciled there for the requisite period, but I haven't had time with one thing and another . . .' Angela began to laugh helplessly. 'Do you find it funny to live in sin?'

That sent her into fresh mirth. 'Oh, Clive, you idiot,' she cried when she could speak, 'was that all it was? The church gave us its blessing, which was quite enough to be going on with.'

'I never dreamed you'd take it like this,' he said with obvious relief. 'I thought you might imagine I'd taken advantage of your innocent trust, so I . . . kept away from you. That's what I meant when I asked you to be patient, I really was on the point of trying to get a special licence . . . our children must be perfectly legitimate.'

'Then you'd better get it quickly, Clive, or you'll be too late,' Angela told him, her eyes sparkling.

He stared at her incredulously with a dawning light in his eyes.

'You don't mean——?'

She nodded. 'And that being so, you needn't keep your distance any longer.'

'Oh, my precious waif!' His arms closed round her, and all the doubts Angela had been harbouring about his feelings for her were drowned in the ardour of his kiss.

Celia Stratton recovered, though she would always limp a little on one leg, but she declared that she could not bring herself to live in the same house as Edmund Sullivan's daughter, which made it easy for Clive to fix her up in a boarding house on the south coast, without having to tell her he had no intention of allowing her to return to Abbotswood. Angela had decided that it would be kinder to keep Jack Forest's revelations to herself, for Clive seemed indifferent and even if she could have made any impression upon Celia's obsession, it would be cruel to undeceive her.

The one thing Celia asked for from Abbotswood was Jasmine's portrait, and this they were only too pleased to send to her.

Clive and Angela stood together watching the lorry taking the crate in which it was packed move down the drive. Clive remarked:

'I'm glad that's gone.'

'So am I,' Angela agreed. 'While that was here I always felt that she was still in the house. But she was very lovely.' She sighed regretfully. 'I wish for your sake I was half as beautiful.'

Clive looked down at her with a tender light in his eyes.

'To me you've always been much more beautiful, for your clear, candid soul is mirrored in your face. All those things I said about despising women were prompted by Jasmine's poison. She definitely ought to have been shut up in a seraglio, where her talent would have had full scope. At large among civilised society, she was a public menace. I didn't regret her.'

'But you loved her once?'

He shook his head. 'That wasn't love. I never knew what love was, didn't believe in it, until I married you.'

Hand in hand they went into the house, which since her portrait had gone seemed cleansed of Jasmine's presence.

'At last I feel this is home,' Angela said.

Clive slipped his arm about her waist. 'Your home, my home, and our children's home,' he told her. 'I shall go no more a-roaming, my beloved. All I want is here.'

THE OMNIBUS
Has Arrived!

A GREAT NEW IDEA
From HARLEQUIN

OMNIBUS

The 3-in-1 HARLEQUIN — only $1.95 per volume

Here is a great new exciting idea from Harlequin. THREE GREAT ROMANCES — complete and unabridged — BY THE SAME AUTHOR — in one deluxe paperback volume — for the unbelievably low price of only $1.95 per volume.

We have chosen some of the finest works of world-famous authors and reprinted them in the 3-in-1 Omnibus. Almost 600 pages of pure entertainment for just $1.95. A TRULY "JUMBO" READ!

The following pages list some of the exciting novels in this series.

Climb aboard the Harlequin Omnibus now! The coupon below is provided for your convenience in ordering.

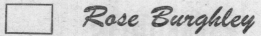

Rose Burghley

Omnibus

Through the years, devoted readers have become familiar with Rose Burghley's inimitable style of writing. And in the best tradition of the romantic novel, all her delightfully appealing stories have captured the very essence of romantic love.

. . . . CONTAINING

MAN OF DESTINY . . . Caroline was a compassionate and loving governess, whose only thoughts concerned the happiness of the neglected little boy in her care. But in the eyes of Vasco Duarte de Capuchos, Caroline's affectionate manner, and indeed Caroline herself, were far removed from his idea of a governess, and of a woman . . . (#960).

THE SWEET SURRENDER . . . the local Welsh folk knew it as Llanlyst, Castle of the Watching Eyes. When Paul Hilliard agreed to accompany her employer to this completely isolated castle on the coast, she had certain misgivings. The unexplained events that followed convinced her she had made a serious mistake . . . (#1023).

THE BAY OF MOONLIGHT . . . Sarah Cunninghame was a very attractive and graceful young woman. Philip Saratola was a distinguished, handsome man. But from the very beginning, their "accidental" relationship was bedevilled by misunderstandings. And the aggressive young Frank Ironside was determined that there would never be a relationship of any kind between them . . . (#1245).

only $1.95

Iris Danbury

Omnibus

Iris Danbury's popular and widely read novels have earned her a place high on the list of everyone's favorites. Her vital characterizations and choice of splendid locations have combined to create truly first class stories of romance.

. . . . CONTAINING

RENDEZVOUS IN LISBON . . . Janice Bowen entered Mr. Everard Whitney's office to inform him she no longer wished to work for him. When she left, her head reeled from the thought of accompanying him on a business trip to Lisbon. This was the first of many times that this impossible man was to astonish her . . . (#1178).

DOCTOR AT VILLA RONDA . . . Nicola usually ignored her sister's wild suggestions, but this one had come at the perfect time. Lisa had asked Nicola to join her in Barcelona. A few days after receiving the letter, Nicola arrived in Spain to discover that her sister had mysteriously disappeared — six weeks before she had written . . . (#1257).

HOTEL BELVEDERE . . . the fact that Andrea's aunt was head housekeeper at the large luxury hotel was sure to create ill feeling among her fellow employees. Soon after Andrea began work, their dangerous jealousy caused untold complications in Andrea's life — and in that of the hotel's most attractive guest . . . (#1331).

only $1.95

Amanda Doyle

Omnibus

To conceive delightful tales and to master the art of conveying them to literally thousands of readers are the keys to success in the world of fiction. Amanda Doyle is indeed a master, for each one of her outstanding novels is considered truly a work of art.

. . . . CONTAINING

A CHANGE FOR CLANCY . . . Clancy Minnow and her manager, Johnny Raustmann, were very happy running the Brenda Downs ranch in Australia. When the trustees appointed a new manager, Clancy had to break the news to Johnny. But Johnny Raustmann had a way out of this — for both of them . . . (#1085).

PLAY THE TUNE SOFTLY . . . when Ginny read the advertisement, it was the answer to both her prayers and her much needed independence. Immediately, she applied to the agency and was soon on her way to Noosa Homestead. But her brief happiness was shattered when she found that her new employer was none other than Jas Lawrence . . . (#1116).

A MIST IN GLEN TORRAN . . . after two years in Paris, Verona finally recovered from the death of her fiancé, Alex Mackinnon. When she returned to her Highland home, there were many changes at Glen Torran. But she discovered that Alex's younger brother, Ewan, still felt the estates he would inherit included Verona . . . (#1308).

only $1.95